"You'd make a good dad.

"Why didn't you and Aunt Erin have more kids?"

If it hadn't been a nine-year-old kid asking him that question, Lance might've lashed out. Instead, Lance gave him a squeeze, trying to find the right words without breaking down. Out of the corner of his eye, Lance glanced at Erin. A tear ran down her cheek, and he watched as she quickly brushed it away.

Lance gave Dylan another squeeze. "Thank you. That's high praise, coming from a wise kid. I'll tell you what. Why don't you leave these grown-up matters to the grown-ups?"

When he'd come to the ranch, he'd been angry with Erin for suggesting that she might find love again and start a new family. But the longing on her face after Dylan's comment was real. He'd made Lily's loss all about him, but after last night, and now, he could see how wrong he'd been.

But he hadn't been able to be the man she'd wanted then...needed then. So what made him think he could be now?

Danica Favorite loves the adventure of living a creative life. She loves to explore the depths of human nature and follow people on the journey to happily-ever-after. Though the journey is often bumpy, those bumps refine imperfect characters as they live the life God created them for. Oops, that just spoiled the ending of Danica's stories. Then again, getting there is all the fun. Find her at danicafavorite.com.

Books by Danica Favorite

Love Inspired

Three Sisters Ranch

Her Cowboy Inheritance
The Cowboy's Faith
His Christmas Redemption

Love Inspired Historical

Rocky Mountain Dreams
The Lawman's Redemption
Shotgun Marriage
The Nanny's Little Matchmakers
For the Sake of the Children
An Unlikely Mother
Mistletoe Mommy
Honor-Bound Lawman

Visit the Author Profile page at Harlequin.com for more titles.

His Christmas Redemption

Danica Favorite

ISBN-13: 978-1-335-47953-2

His Christmas Redemption

This edition published by arrangement with Love Inspired Books.

www.Harlequin.com

Printed in U.S.A.

Blessed are they that mourn:
for they shall be comforted.
—*Matthew* 5:4

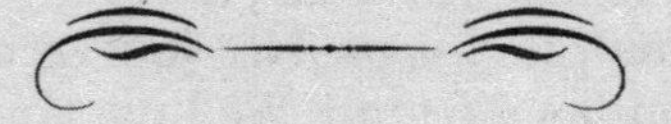

To Connor Dugan, you have become
such an important part of our family.
You have walked alongside us through some
good times and some hard ones, as well.
You mean the world to us, and I'm so grateful
for all you've done for us. Not just as a horseman,
but as a friend. We love you.

Chapter One

Lance Drummond had never expected to find himself on his ex-wife's doorstep. But he'd also never expected that his entire future would hinge upon her. At least not since their divorce. After all, they'd divorced for a reason. Not his reasons, but when someone told you they didn't want to be married to you anymore, and counseling wasn't working, the gentlemanly thing to do was to let that person out.

Besides, wasn't there a saying that if you loved someone, you should set them free? He'd set Erin free, but sometimes his heart told him he was the biggest of all fools. Not just in letting her go, but for still wanting her in the first place. He'd had reasons of his own to want out of the marriage. But where he came from, when you made someone a promise before God and your family, you kept it. He might not have a great relationship with God these days, but he still didn't think it was a good idea to break the promises you made Him. So here he was, knocking on the front door of a woman who'd given up on him, needing her help and not sure how to ask for it.

The door opened and a familiar but much more mature face peered out. “Uncle Lance? What are you doing here? Aunt Erin said you guys got divorced.”

That was one of the worst things about divorce. It wasn’t just about losing the partner who promised to stand by you, no matter what, but also losing extended family you’d grown to love. Like his nephew Dylan. He and Dylan had spent a lot of time together in the past, and the little guy, though not so little anymore at nine years old, used to follow him around.

Lance shook his head. He couldn’t think about those happy times. Not when they were lost to him and he would never get them back.

“We did, bud. But I need to talk to Erin about some things. If she’s home.”

The details were fuzzy when it came to what was going on with Erin and her sisters, Nicole and Leah. Based on the few conversations he’d had with her, they’d inherited some ranch from a relative he’d never heard of and moved to this tiny town of Columbine Springs, in the middle of nowhere Colorado, to make a go of ranching. It had been none of his business, but it seemed kind of foolish for them to pursue something like that when none of them knew the first thing about ranches. But here they were, a year and a half later, and they’d stuck it out.

How they were making it, he wasn’t sure. Erin had called him a few times since their divorce, asking if they could revisit the idea of selling the house they still jointly owned because she needed the money. The most recent call came a couple of weeks ago, but he’d refused, as always.

Why would she think he’d ever be willing to sell?

The house was technically marital property, which the court said had to be split evenly between them, even though he'd paid for most of it. Erin had said he could take his time with either selling the house or buying her out.

One day he'd have the money to buy her out and then his last tie to Erin would be severed.

Dylan held the door open wider. "She's in the kitchen."

Leaving the door open, Dylan ran in the direction of the other room. Though the outside of the house wasn't yet decorated, stepping inside was like entering a Christmas nightmare. Erin and her sisters had always loved the holiday and, when they'd been married, her need to decorate to the hilt had been one of their common disagreements. He hated the commercialism and constant need for more, and she bought every sparkly Christmas item she set her eyes on. She used to want to start decorating as early as possible, but he'd always made her wait until after Thanksgiving.

How early had she started this year? He shook his head. None of his business.

Erin appeared in the doorway, wiping her hands on a towel. Her dark hair was up in a ponytail with random hairs that spilled out all over in the crazy way they did when she was working hard on a project. He shouldn't care about her appearance or how life had been treating her over the past two years. And yet he couldn't help thinking about how good she looked. Happy. Healthy.

Part of him was happy for her. But another part of him wanted to scream at her and ask how she could be doing so well after everything that had happened.

"Lance. What brings you here? Have you finally decided to sell the house?"

"No. But I do need to talk to you about something else. Can we go somewhere private to talk?"

Erin looked around for a moment then shook her head. "I'm afraid not. Leah and Nicole are both on their honeymoons, so I'm taking care of the boys until they get back."

Lance stared at her for a moment. Leah and Nicole on honeymoons?

"Didn't Leah's husband and Nicole's fiancé just die?"

Erin shrugged. "It's been more than two years since Leah's husband died, and it's coming up on two years since Nicole's fiancé died. I'd like to think that they've earned their chance to be happy. They're both very good men, and the double wedding ceremony was one of the most beautiful I've ever seen. Maybe some people think two years is too soon, but when the heart finds what it's looking for, why make it wait longer?"

The longing in her voice was like a knife to his stomach. "Does that mean you've moved on, too?"

Erin let out a long sigh. "Please don't tell me you came all this way to ask about my dating life. It's none of your business. But if you must know, I haven't given up on the idea of falling in love again and having a family."

Having a family? How could she think about that now?

"What about…?" He left a long pause. He hadn't spoken their daughter's name in months and barely at all over the past couple of years. Not since she'd died. Even now just thinking about her put his stomach in knots.

"It doesn't make me love Lily any less," she said, emphasizing Lily's name, like she knew how much it still hurt him to hear it. That was why they could never go back, why he hadn't fought Erin on the divorce. They hadn't seen eye to eye on how to move forward after the tragedy and this, the first conversation they'd had about it in two years, only made it more obvious.

Erin gave him a gentle smile. "Her death was the hardest thing that ever happened to me, but her life was the best. You can't have life without death, and it's worth the pain of death to enjoy the beauty of life."

That was why he'd never been able to talk to her about any of it. Losing their daughter had hurt so much that all he'd wanted to do was to yell and scream or punch something. But she would just go on with her ridiculous notions about thinking positive and those weird Bible verses about hope. Hope wouldn't bring their daughter back. He supposed that was the only way Erin could deal with the pain, considering it was her fault their daughter had died.

Erin stepped forward and placed a hand on his arm. "Is that why you're here? To fight with me over the past, because somehow fighting keeps it, and Lily, alive?"

Her touch burned his arm, but much as he wanted to shove her away and tell her she didn't understand, it also felt so good that he wanted to stay like this forever. That was the trouble with sorting out his feelings over their daughter's death and their failed marriage. He hated Erin on so many levels, but somehow he couldn't stop loving her.

When he didn't answer, she continued. "I know you're struggling with moving on. I'm sorry. I know you didn't like the therapist we went to, but maybe you should consider talking to someone else. It's not healthy for you to still be so stuck in the past."

He stepped away. If one more person said that to him, he would… Well, he didn't know what he would do, but it was like an explosion building up inside him, only there wasn't any place for it to go.

"I am seeing a therapist," he said. "That's why I'm here. I'm supposed to talk to you and make peace with what happened between us."

That wasn't all of it, but for now it would have to be enough. He wasn't even sure that he knew what making peace meant. His counselor said that it was different for everyone, but Lance had to find a way to make the feelings of agony inside his stomach go away and for him to stop talking of Erin and their past with such bitterness. One more thing he didn't know how to accomplish, but the counselor had suggested that talking to Erin might give him a path to figuring it out.

He wasn't sure how much he was going to tell her yet, though. His business partner, Chad Maxwell, was threatening to force him out if he didn't get a counselor to sign off on his mental health. According to Chad, Lance's grief was keeping him from adequately performing his duties in helping him run the outdoor gear company they'd built together from the ground up.

Erin hated the company, and hated Chad even more. She had no idea what either of them meant to Lance, which had been a huge source of conflict in their marriage. So to tell her that he needed this to keep Chad from forcing him out would probably only give her more reason to show him the door.

She gave a casual shrug as if none of it mattered. "I'm at peace with you. I've got nothing against you, and I wish you nothing but the best in life. I'm sorry that you're having a hard time moving forward, but I don't know what that has to do with me."

Before he could answer, a little boy came running into the room. "Auntie Erin! I finished painting my snowman!"

As it dawned on him who the boy was, all the air rushed out of Lance's lungs. Ryan. The little boy was just a few months younger than their daughter had been. He was four now, and Lily…eternally two. Ryan had once been a fixture in their home, and even though the kids had been young, they'd been close. Lance had once loved the little boy like his own. This pain was deeper than what he'd felt at seeing Dylan.

"Who is that?" Ryan asked.

It did not seem right that Ryan didn't remember him.

"This is Lance and he's…" Erin didn't finish her sentence, like she didn't how to explain their relationship to the little boy.

Dylan joined them. "That's Uncle Lance."

Ryan looked confused. "How do we have an uncle Lance? Aunt Nicole is married to Uncle Nando, so did you get married, too?"

Erin let out a long sigh. "He's not my husband anymore."

Obviously they didn't spend much time rehashing family history. Did Erin think of him at all? Of their daughter? She'd moved on and built this happy little life without them.

"Why not?" Ryan's innocent question made Lance feel sick.

She looked uncomfortable and for that he was glad. At least she showed signs of the divorce having some impact on her.

Lance was supposed to be there to find peace, to get closure on this part of his life so he could move on with his future. Erin seemed to have done that, but instead of making him feel better, it only made him feel worse.

Lance had picked a fine time to decide to make peace with her about the past. If he wanted it so badly, why hadn't he just gone ahead and put their house on the market, like she'd asked him to a couple of weeks ago? This was not a discussion she wanted to have in front of the boys, and as Ryan still looked at her expectantly about why she wasn't married anymore, Erin had no idea what to say.

Finally she squatted beside Ryan and put her arm around him. "It's one of those complicated grown-up things," she said. "We used to be married and now we're not."

Ryan tilted his head. "Why not? When Mom and Dad got married, Dad promised he would love us forever and ever and ever, and he would never leave us. Isn't that what you're supposed to do when you get married? How can you not be married anymore?"

Erin sighed. This wasn't an easy topic for a four-year-old to understand. Especially since Leah, his mom, and Shane, his new dad, had just gotten married. It was easy to believe in forever on the day you spoke those vows. But tragedy had a way of changing things. How to explain those complications to a boy who'd been part of a wedding where he was finally getting an amazing dad?

"In most cases, yes. But sometimes bad things happen and the best thing is for both of you to go your separate ways."

Ryan gave her a funny look. "That's not what Mom says. Mom says you have to work together to figure it out. Even if it's hard, Mom says it's worth it in the end to work through your problems. Just like I did with Dylan when he broke my fire truck."

She was rusty at this parenting thing. Being an aunt was so much easier.

Even though they'd all been living in this house together after moving here a year and a half ago, and before that, crammed into Nicole's tiny apartment when Erin had left Lance two years ago, they had been an extended family for as long as Ryan had been alive. Erin tried just to be the boys' aunt and not their mom. This whole conversation felt like a mom discussion, but Leah was on her honeymoon.

So she took a deep breath and prayed that she was using the right words, especially since she could feel Lance's eyes boring into her, demanding that she answer not just for Ryan, but for him. He hadn't wanted the divorce, and it was clear, from his presence, he still didn't understand. But how were you supposed to keep explaining that you couldn't handle being blamed for your daughter's death? Or that he'd been too emotionally unavailable to work through their shared grief together? And why would he want to remain married to her, believing that about her?

Erin hugged Ryan close to her. "You're right. People

should try to work out their problems. Lance and I tried very hard to do so, but unfortunately it didn't work."

She didn't look at Lance as she spoke the words, knowing it would probably just set him off. He didn't want to hear about her pain, but he'd needed someone to blame and be angry at. That's what their counselor had said.

Lance didn't seem angry now, though. Just…lost.

Erin wasn't sure she was the right person to help him find his way again.

Thinking about that time gave her an idea as to how to explain it to Ryan, though. "You remember how you guys went to a counselor when we first came here? Then again, once your mom and Shane decided to get married? Sometimes counselors help you fix things, but sometimes they show you things are too broken to be fixed."

Lance made a strangled noise and Erin looked up to see the sadness in his eyes. He'd stormed out of so many of their counseling sessions. Did he understand just how much of that contributed to the breakdown of their marriage?

It didn't matter. They were divorced now and whatever peace Lance was looking for, she hoped he found it. Even if she wasn't part of that solution.

However her words seemed to resonate with Ryan, who nodded. "I didn't know they did that. Does this mean he can't play with me?"

She looked over at Lance, who seemed extremely uncomfortable. After Lily's death, he couldn't stand being around Ryan, who had spent so much time with them. When things were really bad with Jason, Leah's late husband, Leah would often leave the boys with Erin. In some ways, Ryan and Lily had been like brother and sister.

"I'm not sure if he knows how to play your games," Erin said. "Besides, we have to finish making and putting up our Christmas decorations." Hopefully it would give Lance a way out without looking or feeling like a jerk.

"He could help," Ryan offered.

Given that Erin and her sisters used to jokingly call Lance "the Grinch" because of how he'd make fun of all their Christmas merriment and holiday décor everywhere, asking him to help would probably be the quickest way to get rid of him.

"That's a great idea," Erin said, looking over at Lance. "We haven't gotten the outside lights up yet, and I was wondering how I'd do that all by myself."

Was it wrong of her to get a sick thrill at the look of horror on his face?

As his brow furrowed, she couldn't help smiling. Lance was as good as gone.

Not that she necessarily had anything against him. But what did they have to say to one another anymore? He'd made it clear he didn't want to sell the house.

"I guess I could lend a hand," Lance finally said, sounding like he'd rather have all his toenails pulled out one by one.

Whatever this making peace business was about, it had to be big.

"Great," Erin said, gesturing to a large box in the hall. "If you don't mind carrying that outside, I'll grab a ladder."

When she returned to the front porch, carrying the

ladder, Lance had already opened the box of lights and was looking through them.

"You're going to need to test them," he said.

"Already did that during our Christmas movie marathon over Thanksgiving."

Lance groaned and Erin grinned. Most families were into football games and parades, but Erin and her sisters hated sports, so they'd created their own tradition by watching their favorite Christmas movies. This year their tradition had been slightly abbreviated since they'd been busy with wedding preparations for her sisters' early December wedding.

All their decorating energy had been poured into the wedding and they hadn't had time to get to the house.

That left the job to Erin. She was hoping that by the time her sisters got back from their respective honeymoons in two weeks, the entire place would be transformed into a Christmas wonderland.

As Erin got the ladder situated on the corner of the porch, she couldn't help smiling as she pictured their faces at seeing how Erin had made it their best yet. They'd had so many terrible Christmases over the past few years, with Erin's tragedy and the troubles of Leah's previous marriage. Prior to that, growing up under the iron fist of their father, the Colonel—a man who made Scrooge look like a humanitarian—Christmas hadn't been a joyous occasion in their home. She and her sisters had always promised each other that when they were finally on their own, and had the means to do so, they were going to have the most amazing Christmases ever.

Last year, things had looked like they were going to finally work out for them after all their tragedies.

But Erin had gotten sick, and many of their plans had fallen through. This year Erin was determined. After all these years of waiting, her family would finally have the perfect Christmas they'd always dreamed of. She'd put together a whole binder for the family's perfect Christmas, listing everything they were going to do to celebrate the holiday. She and the boys had spent all afternoon making more decorations, and while they may not be like the ones people bought in stores, her sisters would love knowing how the boys had helped.

She gestured to the string of lights Lance had started unwinding. "Can you hand me that one? And the stapler that's in the box?"

As he handed them to her, he said, "You want me to do that? I used to always..."

He used to always be the one to hang the lights. And at some point during the process, he'd grumpily tell her that she was using more than she had the previous year and that it was a good thing he loved her. They'd end up laughing and kissing, and even though he hated her decorations, it had made her feel so loved that he'd indulged her anyway.

"I learned how to do it myself," she said, taking the stapler in one hand and the lights in the other.

The pain in his eyes told her that he remembered their past, too.

Maybe whatever peace he had to make with her would be good for them both. She'd thought she was over him. After all their conversations once they decided to divorce, she'd thought about how good it was that they were divorced because they could never agree on anything.

But the thing was, even when they'd disagreed during their marriage, they'd often found ways to compromise, making sure the other person had what they needed. Somehow they'd lost that.

As Erin attached the lights to the edge of the roof, she wondered how she could convince Lance to understand that selling the house wasn't about forgetting their daughter. It hadn't meant anything to him while she was alive, so why did he have to put so much importance on it now?

Sometimes she thought it was his way of punishing her for Lily's death. He blamed Erin and, based on their conversations since, he still did. Erin had fallen asleep while Lily napped and hadn't heard Lily wake up. Nor had she heard Lily open the door and go outside. Erin had been so deeply asleep that she hadn't realized her daughter had drowned in the creek until hours later, after discovering Lily missing. A search party had found the body.

She should have done a better job getting Lily to understand the dangers of playing by the creek. The little girl had been fascinated by the rushing water and went there every chance she got. Erin should have double-checked the lock on the door to make sure it was locked. She should have told Lance she wasn't feeling well and that was why she hadn't wanted him going back to work that day, instead of picking a fight with him and complaining that he spent more time at work than with his family. She should have…

Erin wiped a tear from her face. So many should haves, and not one would bring their daughter back. Nor would it bring back the baby she'd been carrying at the time. She hadn't even had the chance to tell Lance, which was probably a good thing since he'd likely blame her for that loss, as well. More moisture hit her face and she realized it wasn't tears. The storm forecast to hit tonight was blowing in earlier than expected. Just a few more feet and she'd have this part done.

"Hey," Lance called up. "It's starting to snow. Maybe you should save this for another day."

"I know," she said. "I just need to finish this section."

He made a noise like he always did when he was going to argue, but he didn't say anything.

A few more snowflakes hit her face and a gust of wind blew the string still hanging. If she didn't get it secured, the storm would likely rip the whole thing off and not only would she have to redo the lights, she'd probably have to buy new ones. They'd made that mistake last year when they started decorating early in the season.

She put an extra couple of staples in the section then climbed down. "Help me move this so I can get the last part."

Lance made his annoyed noise again. "Why don't you let me do it?"

Maybe it was petty, but this was typical Lance, not approving of her actions but then stepping in to do it for her to show how magnanimous he was.

"I've got it, thanks," she said, moving the ladder and returning to her position.

"It'll take you two trips up and down and moving the ladder again. I've got a longer reach."

Technically true. But she was already up.

The first staple went in strong and satisfying. That was the other reason she wanted to do this. Maybe it would help him make peace with the past to see just how much she no longer needed him. As Erin pulled the next section of lights toward her, reaching to where she wanted to place it, her foot slipped. The metal ladder was getting slippery with the snow coming down. She probably should have let Lance do this one. He'd been right about her reach and she wouldn't risk another trip up and down again.

Maybe if she secured the end instead of leaving it hanging loose, she could come back another day and re-fasten it. She tugged at the end, which had gotten caught on one of the rungs.

"Be careful," Lance said.

She pulled on the end again, trying to angle it out of where it was caught. Her trick worked, freeing the strand.

She spied one of the hooks they'd used last year to put wooden cutouts on the roof. The cutouts hadn't lasted beyond the first storm, but this remaining hook was perfect for looping the last of the string and securing it. However, as she reached for it, her foot slipped again. It wasn't until she was on her way to the ground that she realized just how seriously she'd misjudged the distance.

Her arm holding the stapler hit the ladder and it seemed weird to notice that she was still holding her stapler. Especially since, when she hit the ground, she was pretty sure there were three Lances staring down at her.

Lance had gotten Erin to the hospital as quickly as he could. It was obvious, even without a doctor looking at it, she'd likely broken both her right arm and her left foot. Based on some of the strange things she'd said, he was also pretty sure she had a concussion. As an avid outdoorsman, he was well-versed in first aid.

The boys had brought along some books and games. It was hard watching them interact and wondering if this could have been his life, too. He and Erin had planned on having other children, but they hadn't been so fortunate, and maybe that was for the best.

Ryan came over and handed him a book. "Will you read to me? I'm bored with coloring."

The little boy didn't wait for a response but climbed up into his lap. "You might not be my uncle anymore, but I like you. I hope you do the voices better than Uncle Nando."

Was it getting warmer in the waiting room? His throat felt like sandpaper as he opened the book and tried to read. How hard was it to say "The Amazing World of Dinosaurs"? But it physically hurt his throat to try.

"You can read, can't you?" Ryan asked. He pointed to a word. "That one says 'dinosaur.' Dylan says I just have it memorized because I read so many dinosaur books. But I actually know how to read. Not all the words, because I haven't gone to school yet. Just preschool."

Maybe Lance should have put on one of those masks they offered at the front door to help stop the spread of germs. He was obviously coming down with something.

"I can read. 'The Amazing World of Dinosaurs,'" Lance said. "But you already know that."

Ryan rewarded him with a wide grin and snuggled closer. It had been more than two years since Lance had held a child in his arms. He took a deep breath, inhaling the warm little-boy scent that hadn't changed all that much. Leah still obviously used the same children's shampoo.

As he started to read, the tightness in Lance's chest relaxed. He glanced at Dylan, who looked up from his book and smiled.

They hadn't gotten very far into their book when the nurse came out.

Lance stood. "Is Erin okay? Can we see her?"

The nurse smiled. "I'm going to bring you back. The doctor would like to keep her overnight for observation. With her injuries, it will be better for her to be where we can watch over her and help her for these first few hours."

The nurse hesitated then continued. "I'll be honest. She's been arguing with us about going home tonight. She is worried about the boys. I asked her if you were a danger to them and she said no. But she's worried about being an imposition. Is that how you feel about her?"

Erin had said the same thing when she'd first asked him to take her to the hospital. What was he supposed to do, leave an injured woman to figure it out herself? Granted they were no longer married, so he didn't owe her anything. But he'd like to think he was still a decent human being who would step in to help whenever someone needed it. He let out a long sigh.

"She's not an imposition. I know she worries about it, but she worries too much. The boys and I will be fine."

The nurse gave him a relieved smile. "That's what I thought would be the response because I passed by here a couple of times and watched you with the boys.

If you'd like a few minutes alone with her to discuss arrangements, I'd be happy to keep them occupied."

He helped the boys gather their things and then the nurse led them into the exam room, where Erin was dressed in a hospital gown, her arm in a cast, her leg in a boot and a sour look on her face. "I think they're overreacting," she said before he even entered. "I'm fine. I just need to be in my own bed."

He studied her face. The strained expression of pain was gone, but when he glanced at the IV they'd put in her, he wondered if they'd given her something for it. She'd probably argued about that, as well, but hopefully it would take the edge off so she could feel better.

"Do you remember hitting your head when you fell?" he asked.

She let out a long sigh. "It all happened so fast. There are pieces of my fall I don't remember."

"That's because you have a concussion," the nurse said, entering the room. She turned to Ryan and Dylan. "I have to go check on the room where your aunt is going to spend the night. Do you boys want to come and give me a hand?"

The boys gave an enthusiastic yes but Lance waited until the door closed behind them before he turned to Erin. "I agree with the nurse that you should spend the night. It's a lot safer for you if you're here, especially given that it's going to be hard getting used to going around in a walking boot, with a cast on your opposite arm, and maintaining your balance."

Erin let out a long sigh. "I don't want to be a bother. I'm not your responsibility anymore."

"Maybe not as my wife, but that doesn't mean I'm not going to help someone in need. The snow hasn't let up. We're all better off staying put for the night, rather than trying to make it over the pass. I saw a sign for a hotel just a block or so away. The boys and I can hunker down, and you can get some rest. Driving home tomorrow will be much safer for us all."

She hated driving in the snow and she hated driving with him in the snow. She thought he drove too fast and took too many risks. He thought she worried too much. He'd never had an accident, but he could use her fear of one to convince her to stay tonight.

"I was worried about that. The roads getting bad, that is." A weary look crossed her face. "You're sure you won't mind taking the boys overnight?"

"I'm not a monster," he said.

He couldn't read the expression on her face as she held her free hand out to him. "Come here."

When he reached her side, she took his hand in hers. "I never thought you were," she said. "We just..." Erin closed her eyes for a moment. "I needed a different level of connection than you could give me. It doesn't make either one of us monsters. We're just not compatible."

A tear ran down her cheek and, for the first time, he wondered if maybe their divorce had been just as hard on her as it had been on him.

But she'd left him. Any regret she might feel at that action was her fault.

She pulled her hand out of his and wiped at her cheek. "Sorry. The medications they gave me are making me emotional. I know how you hate that. Anyway, my concern over being an imposition is that I don't want to make you ruin your plans just because of my clumsiness."

"I don't have any plans," he said.

Now would be the perfect time to explain that Chad had essentially relieved him of his duties at work until he could deal with his grief. But Erin yawned as she nodded slowly. Maybe not. She wasn't in the right frame of mind to discuss anything important.

The door opened and the nurse reentered with the boys. "I know you just got to see her, but she does need her rest and visiting hours are almost over. So say your goodbyes and you can see her in the morning."

Before they could leave, a doctor entered the room. "Good. Your family hasn't left. I was hoping to catch them."

He turned to Lance and held out his hand. "Steve Purcell," he said. "I just want to be sure that when Erin goes home tomorrow, she won't be going home alone."

The doctor explained Erin's injuries to Lance and none of it surprised him. Nor did it come as a shock when the doctor said, "She's not capable of being on her own right now. I can't release her unless I know there's going to be a responsible adult with her in the house to look after the boys. Their mother, perhaps?"

Lance glanced over at Erin, who wore a panicked expression on her face, like she was afraid of what answer he would give.

"The boys' mother is on her honeymoon," Lance said, turning his attention back to the doctor.

"Don't you dare call her." Erin sat straighter in her bed, whatever grogginess she'd been feeling during their conversation seemingly gone. "Leah has been working really hard to save up for this trip. You can't ruin it and make her come home early. I'll be fine. Please."

It was just like Erin to be worried about ruining Leah's honeymoon. Were it anyone else, he would insist on calling. But she was right. If Leah knew that Erin had been injured, she would change her plans and come straight home. He didn't want that for her. Even Lance could admit that his ex-sister-in-law deserved to enjoy her honeymoon.

"Please," Erin said more gently. "I can do this. I'm far more capable than anyone gives me credit for."

"I understand what you're saying," Lance said slowly. "I wouldn't want to ruin Leah's honeymoon, either. I'll stay with you. I'll help with the boys."

She gave him a hopeful look. "You would do that? What about your job?"

He nodded. "I'm on a bit of an extended vacation."

It was the closest to the truth he could give right now, especially in front of all these people.

This time when Erin slumped back against her pillows, all the fight had left her. It had clearly taken all of her energy to protect her sister and now the medication had won.

"All right." She turned to look at the doctor. "You heard him. Lance is going to stay with us. And even though he doesn't have to, I appreciate it. You can fill him in on any necessary information. My sister is back in two weeks and she can take over then."

It was obvious she hadn't wanted to agree to letting him stay but she'd had no other choice. And while spending the next two weeks taking care of Erin wasn't high on Lance's priority list, maybe it would allow him to discover the elusive peace he'd been hoping to find.

As they left the hospital room he took a final glance back at Erin, who was already drifting off to sleep.

He didn’t understand his tender feelings for her at this moment. Maybe it was because she was injured. But he’d do well to remind himself not to let his heart get entangled with hers again.

Chapter Two

"We need to make cookies," Erin said as Lance helped her out of the car when they got back to the ranch the next day.

"You just got home," he said. "Let's get you settled in and maybe, in a few days, we'll give it a go."

Even though Lance had known about Erin's love for Christmas, he hadn't expected she'd want to continue her activities as normal when she got home. But he should have guessed, considering how important it was to her. As he watched the defiant expression cross her face, he knew this wasn't going to be an easy battle.

That had always been the trouble with Erin. When she got something stuck in her mind, it was almost impossible to convince her to see sense. Wasn't that what had gotten her into this position in the first place?

He'd told her to let him finish the lights. Had she listened? No. And in a careless moment she'd been injured. At least this time it was only her safety she'd compromised. But what if he hadn't been able to take care of her? What would she have done with the boys? Would she have had to call her sister home?

Even though everyone told him that Lily's death was nothing more than a tragic accident, Lance knew that if only Erin had been more careful, more responsible, she would have remembered to lock the door and wouldn't have fallen asleep. Maybe then, their daughter would still be alive.

"I'll be fine," she insisted, struggling to get out of her seat.

As much as Erin claimed she felt fine, she'd slept almost the entire drive back to the ranch. He'd had enough injuries of his own to know that a concussion took longer than most people thought to heal. Add in the pain from her fall and she wasn't going to be fine for a long time.

"You've only just gotten out of the hospital, so let's take it one step at a time. Starting with getting you into the house."

He tried not to laugh as she glared at him. It was almost fun, watching her squirm. The look on her face as she glanced down at her foot then up at the stairs leading to the porch was priceless. Though they'd put her in a walking boot, the cast on her right arm would make it difficult for her to grab on to anything for balance.

Plus, it was hard to take her seriously when she was wearing a gaudy Christmas sweater with a giant llama on the front that said, "I llama wish you a Merry Christmas." Her outfit was absolutely ridiculous, but when she was in the hospital, Lance and the boys had stopped at a discount store to buy them all some necessities for their overnight stay, as well as some things for Lance's stay at Erin's, and the boys had insisted that Erin needed that sweater.

She'd accepted the boys' gift with dignity, but he

could tell by the horrified expression on her face that it was a bit much, even for her. Her acceptance of the ugly sweater was one of the many things he'd always loved about her. Erin's warmth always made people feel…

Lance shook his head. There was a big difference between finding peace with their relationship and remembering those feelings. Best to focus on the task at hand.

"Put your arm around my neck," he said, bending beside the car. "You can balance on me until you get the hang of walking in that thing."

She nodded slowly as she scooted out of the seat, putting her arm around him. She'd been in his arms only the day before, when he'd taken her to the hospital, but this felt different. Like… He couldn't put words to it. But he liked the feeling of Erin trusting him and relying on him. They'd once had it and, somehow, they'd lost it.

Once he got her into the house, he took her to the family room. The space was cozy, with couches arranged by a fireplace and half-opened boxes of decorations in the corner. Some of the decorations were already in place but, judging from the boxes, Erin had a lot more to go.

"Is that end of the couch a recliner?" Lance asked. "The nurse said you should keep your foot elevated as much as possible."

"Yes," Erin said. "But I told you, I need to bake cookies today. I have a list, and if I don't stick to the schedule, I won't have everything done by the time my sisters get home. We'll only have a few days before Christmas then, and I don't want them worrying about everything I didn't finish."

Was she kidding? Of course not. Erin didn't kid about Christmas. If the halls weren't decked to the nines, she wasn't happy. And right now, even though most people would call the house decorations perfectly fine, he knew it wasn't up to Erin's standards.

Even though Erin would have hated the comparison, her insistence on perfect Christmas décor reminded him of his mother. The only difference was that his mother always hired professional decorators and hosted parties to show off her efforts.

He could at least be thankful Erin wasn't one to throw a party. How he hated his mother's parties, with all the fake cheer and plastic smiles, pretending to be the perfect family.

At least Erin never pretended things were perfect when they weren't.

"They're going to understand," Lance told her. "You've got a broken ankle and a broken arm. It's not going to kill anyone to not have everything done perfectly. Besides, if you bake the cookies now, they'll be spoiled by Christmas."

"Not if you freeze them," she said, removing her arm from his shoulder. "And just because you hate Christmas doesn't mean the rest of us can't celebrate the way we want."

"I do not hate Christmas," he said through gritted teeth. They'd barely gotten Erin home and already they were starting in to their old patterns. "I just think that all this nonsense isn't necessary. There's nothing wrong with getting some cookies from the bakery, dumping a packet of hot chocolate into a mug of hot water, and sitting in front of a tree that doesn't look like Rudolph vomited on it."

"That's disgusting," Erin said as she stepped away. "And that is exactly the problem between us. I see the beauty in holiday decorations and you want to compare them to animal waste."

At this rate, she was going to take another tumble. Maybe not off a ladder, but it was still going to hurt.

"I just think less is more," he said, trying to sound calm. "It's your house, and you can do whatever you want. But the nurse said you have to stay off that foot and keep it elevated for the first few days."

He held an arm out to her. "Come on, Erin. I don't want to fight. I'm just trying to keep you safe. If having homemade cookies means so much to you, we'll figure it out. After you rest."

Tears filled her eyes. Lance squeezed his eyes shut and started to count to ten. The last thing he needed was for her to start crying on him. Why did she have to be so emotional about everything?

When he got to nine, Erin took his arm. "I just want to have the perfect Christmas."

He opened his eyes and looked at her. "You don't need to have all this stuff for that. Besides, you guys had this place last year. Didn't you get to do everything then?"

"I had the flu. We got the decorating mostly done, but I got sick before I got to enjoy any of it," she said, a sad look crossing her face. "I didn't even get to watch the boys open the hats Shane had bought them. Plus, we got a lot of decorations on clearance after Christmas last year, so this is the first we'll get to use them."

The tone of her voice and the way her forehead was wrinkling made him realize that some of the emotion he was witnessing was sheer exhaustion on her part.

Not only was she injured and on painkillers, she was obviously under a lot of strain—trying to plan the perfect Christmas, taking care of her nephews on her own and now having to deal with him. He might, as she'd often accused him, be low on the emotional intelligence scale, but he could at least tell that what Erin really needed at this point was a nap.

"We'll make it work," he said softly, putting his arm around her and leading her toward the couch. She didn't fight him, just looked up at him sadly.

"If you say so," she said.

Lance got her situated on the couch and the boys came running in the room. "Uncle Lance! Can you play with us?"

"I'm still getting your aunt settled in right now. Why don't you help me by getting her a glass of water so she can take her medicine?"

Erin looked up at him. "I don't want any more painkillers. Leah's first husband died because of a drug overdose that started with a painkiller addiction."

He'd known that, but he hadn't realized just how much it had affected Erin. He'd heard the nurse warn her that the first couple of days out of the hospital she needed to be diligent about taking her medication because they'd had her on such strong medicine in the hospital initially.

"We'll wean you off gradually, just like the nurse said," Lance told her, sitting next to her on the couch. "You're not going to become addicted, but if you don't stay on top of the pain, the nurse said it will get really bad and you'll end up back in the hospital. Is that what you want?"

Erin shook her head. "I know I sound like a bratty

child here, but I don't think you understand just how hard this is for me."

He took her hand and gave it a squeeze. "I think, of all people, I understand the most. I know you hate feeling powerless and it's not like you to sit around and do nothing. But you have to take care of yourself or you're useless for taking care of anyone else. You know that. I promise I'll help you get ready for Christmas."

"You said when we got divorced that you were never celebrating Christmas again."

Not only had he said that but he'd kept his word. He'd never liked how commercial the holiday had become, and hated it even more now that he and Erin were divorced. Every stupid decoration reminded him of the woman who'd loved—and left—him.

But helping Erin didn't mean celebrating. As far as he was concerned, these could just be chores, like cleaning the toilet. He chuckled at the thought. Erin would be so offended if she heard him comparing the two, but at least the thought made the activity palatable.

"What's so funny?" she asked.

The boys came back in the room, so he didn't have to explain. Besides, when he saw what Ryan was holding, Lance didn't feel much like laughing anymore. He'd know that bear anywhere.

"Where did he get that?" Lance looked over at Erin.

"It was Lily's. You and I aren't the only ones who miss her. He doesn't really remember her, but when he was little, he used to cry for his Lily, so I started letting him sleep with her favorite teddy bear. And now it's his."

Ryan squeezed his teddy to his chest. "Her name is Lily. She's my Lily bear."

That's what Erin used to call Lily. Her little Lily bear. Lance had thought it a silly name and now hearing it made his heart ache.

"You gave him Lily's bear?" Lance stared at Erin.

"I did what I thought was best. She's not here to enjoy it, and it makes him happy, so what's wrong with that?"

Lance didn't answer. What was he supposed to say? He couldn't exactly take what was obviously a beloved toy away from Ryan and yet it didn't seem fair.

"I sleep with her every night," Ryan said. "Except for last night, and I really missed her." Ryan squeezed the bear to his chest. "I promise I won't ever leave you again."

"Bears are for babies," Dylan said, handing Erin a glass of water. "Here's your drink, like you asked."

"I'm not a baby. Lily bear is my special friend."

Erin patted the seat next to her. "Of course she is. And we don't think you're a baby." Erin looked over at Dylan. "Apologize to your brother."

"Sorry," Dylan said.

Ryan grabbed a blanket from a nearby chair then climbed up onto the couch and snuggled next to Erin. She put her arm around the little boy in such a maternal way that it made Lance's heart hurt. How many times had he seen her do that with Lily? She'd been that way with both boys, as well, and the thing he'd always appreciated about her was how loving she'd been to all the children.

Lance hadn't had that kind of love growing up. His parents, not the touchy-feely type, were more interested in showing off the trophies of their children's accomplishments. Just like with Christmas. It wasn't about celebrating the reason for the season, but about impressing their neighbors and clients. He'd always promised himself that if he had children, they'd be part of a loving family. He thought they'd given that to Lily; one of the small comforts he'd had with her short life. As much as he hadn't wanted the divorce, sometimes he wondered if Erin had been right in pursuing it, given that he didn't think they were capable of loving each other that way anymore.

Erin whispered something in Ryan's ear then Ryan looked over at Dylan. "I accept your apology," he said.

Sometimes it was easy to forget the things Lance had against Erin, especially when he was reminded of the kind and loving woman she was. He just didn't know how that translated to being at peace with her. His counselor had told him that he needed to forgive Erin for what happened to Lily. But as much as Lance wanted to believe that Erin had learned from her mistakes, it was clear she still didn't always think her decisions through.

If she were responsible, and thought about things logically, she wouldn't be arguing with him over taking care of herself. She'd be more focused on getting well and taking care of the children than on some crazy idea of what she thought Christmas was supposed to be like.

Erin looked up at him. "If you can get me my pain pills, I should go ahead and take one now, before the pain gets worse. If you don't mind, I'd also like you to put on a movie for Ryan and me to watch. Neither of us slept well last night, so we're just going to veg out in front of the TV."

Ryan cradled the bear in his arms as he tucked the blanket around him and Erin. It was a cozy picture. As much as Lance wanted to nurse the feelings of hurt, his heart melted a little when Ryan bent and kissed the top of his bear's head.

Lily was dead. What did it matter that her bear was providing comfort to another child?

Once Erin was settled with her movie, Lance got out his laptop. Even though he was technically on a leave of absence, he still liked to keep up on as much as he could. But he found, as the cartoon character of Ebenezer Scrooge came on the screen, he was more focused on the movie than on his work. Erin would probably have something to say about that, but when he turned to look at her, she'd already fallen asleep. Cuddled with the little boy, she was the picture of everything he wished his life could have been had it not been cruelly taken from him.

Maybe what people didn't understand about Lance, or about these famous characters of Christmas, was that their perceived badness didn't happen in a vacuum. There were reasons for the pain, and it wasn't so simple to just get over it, as everyone seemed to want them to do. Maybe it happened in the movies, but the people in the movies didn't wake up every morning to an emptiness that nothing could ever fill.

His counselor wanted him to make peace with Erin. He still didn't know what that meant, but he'd like to think that when he talked to her next, and he told her about taking care of Erin, she'd see this as doing just that. Surely taking care of the person who'd done the most to hurt you was a sign that you'd made peace with your past.

When Erin woke, there was a fire in the fireplace, the television was off and the boys were gone. This was why she hadn't wanted to take the pain medicine. It made her too sleepy and she couldn't pay attention or keep track of the boys.

Lance used to ask her how he would know that she had learned from her mistake and would never fall asleep while watching a child again. She hadn't had an answer at the time, but living with Leah and her boys, she was always on edge if she was supposed to be watching them. True, Lance was there, but sometimes she felt that he looked at her like he was just waiting for her to mess up again. Leah often told her that even Mary lost track of a young Jesus when he went off to go preach in the synagogue. Surely if the mother of the son of God didn't always do it right then Erin could give herself a break, as well.

Just try telling that to Lance. She shifted her weight, trying to see the best way to scoot herself off the couch and move around. She could hear laughter coming from the kitchen. It seemed selfish to spoil their fun by calling out for them. But no sooner had she flipped the lever to put the foot of the recliner down than Lance stepped into the living room, wearing the reindeer apron the boys had purchased for her last Christmas.

"Let me help you," he said.

"What are you guys doing in there?"

He shrugged. "Making cookies. The boys showed me a Christmas binder, and while I know you want to be part of the cookie-making process, there are a lot of cookies to be baked, so we went ahead and started. What do you need to make so many Christmas cookies for, anyway?"

Lance had started making the cookies? "You don't

know how to make anything that doesn't come out of a box."

"They say necessity is the mother of invention. It's too expensive to eat out all the time, and I don't like eating frozen dinners day in and day out. So I watched a few videos on the internet and, while I'll never be a chef, I won't starve."

"You were good at grilling," she said. Then she added, "Our church has refreshments every Sunday after the service. But they also like to do something a little special for the holidays. Baking cookies relaxes me, so I volunteered to do extra this year. I'm just glad my day to bring them wasn't today. At least we'll have them for next week."

She tried not to sound discouraged as she spoke. Before her nap, she'd sounded so whiny that she'd gotten on her own nerves. Even now she was trying not to let the situation get the best of her. It had been a silly accident and she needed to find a way to look on the bright side.

"I didn't realize you started going to church again," he said.

He looked like he was going to add something argumentative but then he stopped. The counselor had recommended they go to church together, but Lance had informed her that he saw no point in chasing after a God who could be so cruel as to take their child from them.

"It's been a great way for us to get involved in our community. Pastor Roberts is a wonderful teacher and we've all grown a lot closer to the Lord thanks to him. I've never been part of a place where the people were so warm and welcoming."

The hesitation on his face was confirmation of just how far apart they'd grown and why she couldn't see them having a future together. Maybe, for all the doubts she'd had about their divorce, having him there now was what she needed as confirmation of what had truly become important in her life.

"I don't believe in God anymore," he said.

Erin took a deep breath. "I know. But that's something for the two of you to work out. If you'd rather not help with the cookies, I understand. Even though everyone I know is busy with their own holiday preparations, I'm sure I can find someone to help me."

Though she'd put a cheerful tone in her voice, she knew that many of the people from church already had too many commitments on their plates. She'd ended up signing up to make extra because they hadn't had enough people who could do it.

"It's just cookies," he said. "It's not like I have to go—" He stopped. "I'm going to have to take you to church, aren't I?"

She honestly hadn't thought that far ahead. She would like to go to church, but she was already asking a lot of Lance. She'd seen the look on his face when she'd explained about Lily's bear becoming Ryan's.

"I'll try to find a ride. My boss, Ricky, drives right past here on his way. If he can't pick us up, maybe you could just drop us off and then go have a cup of coffee and pastry. There's a great café in town that has the best bear claws."

Lance gave her a funny look. "I like bear claws."

If it were anyone but Lance, she'd have hugged him. It wasn't that she didn't want to hug him, but because it was Lance, she wasn't sure she'd be able to leave his arms after being in them again. She'd already struggled with it when he'd brought her into the house. It was hard being so close to someone she'd loved for so long…their relationship was now so different.

He helped her into the kitchen, where the boys were making shapes out of dough. It wouldn't have been her first choice, but she could see Lance's laptop perched on the counter with the video paused.

How was she supposed to remain immune to him? That's what she'd never been able to understand about Lance. How could you not like a man who didn't know how to cook, hated Christmas, but was willing to go online and watch videos to learn how to bake Christmas cookies for a woman in need?

"Here, Auntie Erin," Ryan said, handing her a glob of dough. "You have to make it into candy cane shapes."

As she got closer, she realized that they had white and red dough that they were making into ropes and then twisting into a candy cane shape.

"Candy cane cookies?" she asked. "I haven't had these in ages."

"You used to make these cookies—"

When we were married. At least that's what Erin thought Lance was about to say. He used to tell her that they were his favorite cookies. His grandmother had made them for him. And Erin, wanting to do something nice for him, had made them. Personally she'd never liked them. But she'd always made them for Lance. She hadn't made them since their divorce. There wasn't any point given that Lance had been the only one who'd liked them. She should have known this would have been his default choice. It just hadn't occurred to her how much that choice would affect her.

It was strange, remembering the simple thing she'd done for him to put that look of happiness on his face. He might not understand the big deal about Christmas but, for Erin, the big deal, at least in terms of why all this meant so much to her, was that there was nothing like the expression of joy on someone's face when they realized that you'd taken the time to think of them and do something special for them.

Erin, who had spent so much of her life as the middle child, not being noticed in the same way as her siblings, liked to make sure everyone felt noticed. Important. And Christmas was the perfect time to show people in very special ways what they meant to her.

Lance might think her vision of the perfect Christmas was silly, but he'd never been as sentimental as she was.

While she had never intended for Lance to remain a part of her holiday traditions, God had him there for a reason. Even though she hadn't been able to think of any sort of peace he might need from her or she from him, obviously God had something different in mind for this holiday season. She just prayed that whatever it was, when her sisters returned and life was back to normal, it wouldn't hurt so much to say goodbye to Lance again.

Chapter Three

If Lance hadn't once been married to Erin, he'd have thought her giant Christmas planner a joke. But when it came to Erin and her planners, she was dead serious. The only trouble was, Lance wasn't sure how he was going to accomplish all the items on her list. It was tempting to simply do the items that were easy and skip the rest, but that would mean Erin would just find a way to do them herself.

And judging from the way her face scrunched up in pain when she tried to stretch the time period between medication, her injury was still bothering her a couple days after the accident. It was to be expected, but not when you were Erin and you had a list.

That was why Lance found himself standing on the front porch, wrapped in winter gear after picking up the boys from school. It had remained cold enough after the snow that Erin was determined to check off one of the items on her list—sledding.

The boys ran out from the barn, carrying an old sled. "Here it is, Uncle Lance."

Erin came stomping onto the porch. To go outside,

Lance had layered garbage bags over her boot to keep her foot dry, but it made it more difficult for her to maneuver.

"That hill over there is good for sledding," she said, pointing to a nice area in front of the house. "I can stay here on the porch and watch you guys."

She didn't look happy about it and he didn't blame her. After all, sledding was fun. They'd often gone with friends to a giant hill near their house. The passing thought brought an ache to his heart.

A few months before Erin had gotten pregnant they'd gone sledding together. It had been the most wonderful day and Lance could still remember cuddling by the crackling fire with Erin, talking about how someday they'd bring their kids to do the same.

Only it hadn't ever happened.

Lily had died before she was old enough to enjoy the giant sledding hill.

He glanced over at Erin. Did she remember?

Maybe it didn't matter to her the way it did to him. But remembering, at least for him, was what made it so difficult to move on and find peace. It was easy to go on with his life, being angry with Erin. However his anger was only part of the story. The other part was the great love he'd once had for her and not understanding how it could so easily be gone. How she could just walk away from it. And why, as much as she had hurt him, he could still cling to those memories and wish things had turned out differently.

Dylan handed him the sled. Even though it wouldn't have been Lance's first choice, it looked safe enough. Lance glanced over at Erin.

She gave him a smile and gestured at the hill. "Go

on. I don't know why, but it's always seemed to me that sledding makes it more Christmassy. We don't always have enough snow around Christmas, so I'm excited to give the boys a chance."

Erin sat on the chair he'd brought out for her then took the camera from around her neck and held it up. "Leah will be sad to have missed it, but I'll get some great pictures for her."

When they'd been married, Erin had often told him that a picture couldn't replace being there. She'd been angry with him for all the time he'd spent at work. In their fights leading up to the divorce, she'd mentioned it more than once. Their daughter had just died and she'd wanted to rub it in about all the things he'd missed.

Maybe she was right. But he'd been doing his best, trying to provide a life for their family. He'd always thought that as the business grew, and Lily got older, it would be easier to take the time off that he needed. He just hadn't counted on not having the opportunity to watch his daughter grow up. He'd never thought that the someday he'd been counting on wouldn't ever come.

He swallowed the lump in his throat and looked at the boys. They had picked up some snow and were tossing small snowballs at each other.

Erin must have sensed where his attention had gone. "It's okay. We've talked to the boys about safety and they know it's okay to throw snowballs, as long as they're little ones and you have the other person's permission."

She sounded so prim as she spoke, the great rule enforcer. But the two of them had gotten into enough snowball fights of their own that Lance knew Erin didn't always fight fair.

He bent and picked up a little bit of snow, carefully shaping it into a ball as he walked toward her.

"Don't tell me that's for me," she said, looking at him sternly. "You wouldn't harm a poor, defenseless woman, would you?"

He grinned. "That's never stopped you before."

Erin glanced over at the boys. "That was in the past. And my sisters and I have agreed that all our snowball fights would be fair."

Lance could attest to the sheer brutality of their competitiveness when it came to games and things like snowball fights. That was odd, considering how well they all got along otherwise. If the brothers took after the sisters, Lance could see why they would need to institute rules on fairness.

"But I'm not your sister," he said, coming closer.

"You wouldn't dare."

Until that moment he hadn't been planning on using the snowball against her. But there was something about the gleam in her eyes that felt like an irresistible dare.

He tossed the snowball in her direction. It hit her square in the chest.

Erin jumped up. "You're going to regret that."

She hobbled over to the porch railing and grabbed some of the snow that was still there. It was good snow. The soft, fluffy kind that made for easy packing. It would have been easy to walk away, or at least to dodge her attack. But it had been a long time since Lance had seen that look in her eyes and he'd be a fool if he didn't admit that it was one of the most beautiful things he'd seen in a long time. It wasn't that Erin was pretty. Because pretty wasn't the right word for her. There was something strong, fierce and incredibly awe-inspiring in her eyes. The expression was what had attracted him to Erin in the first place, because he knew that if you were fortunate enough to have the love of a woman like that, you had more than most men ever dreamed of.

A snowball hit him smack in the face.

That was a good reminder of the downside to loving a woman like Erin.

Lance picked up another handful of snow. Erin scooped more from the railing.

"Do you really want to do this?" she asked. "Because I will win."

Snowballs went sailing at the same time and while Erin's hit him square in the chest, his missed.

"You still want to mess with me?" she asked.

"Uncle Lance!" Dylan came running to him. "When we were in the house getting ready, you said we couldn't get Aunt Erin. The snow will hurt her cast."

Ryan followed his brother. "You can't get Auntie!"

The boys both picked up snow and made snowballs that they tossed directly at Lance.

The snow hit Lance with a resounding thud. Erin laughed. "That's what you get for breaking the rules."

Lance shook his head as he brushed the snow off. "I can definitely see where I didn't think that idea through well enough."

"You should say you're sorry and give her a hug," Dylan said, looking at him sternly.

When he looked at Erin, she was still wiping tears of mirth from her eyes and Lance didn't think she'd heard the little boy.

"I don't think that's a good idea, buddy," Lance said.

Innocent eyes looked up at him. "Why not? Mom

says hugs are always a good idea," Dylan said. Then Dylan frowned. "Unless the person doesn't want a hug, and then you should respect their wishes. But auntie loves hugs."

As if his lecture settled the matter, both Dylan and Ryan ran to Erin and hugged her. Erin smiled as she looked over their heads at him. "I do love hugs," she said. "But we don't have to if it makes you uncomfortable. At least now you know that we take our rules very seriously here, and you shouldn't even think about messing with me."

Her tone was light and there was understanding in her eyes. He'd been trying to have fun, they both had, but it was amazing how even the smallest things became difficult reminders of their complicated past. Maybe, even though it seemed like they were both trying to move forward, making peace wasn't as easy as his therapist had led him to believe.

So what did peace look like? What did it mean to come to terms with both their daughter's death and their divorce?

Maybe, as the boys ran back to their sled, it wasn't a question they needed to settle right this very minute.

Lance grinned at Erin. "I will be expecting a rematch once you're healed."

"You're on," she said, laughing.

That was the other thing he'd loved, and missed, about Erin. Her laugh. She had one of the most beautiful, most contagious, laughs of anyone he'd ever met. The kind that made you feel absolutely comfortable and at ease because you knew she was laughing with you, not at you.

"Uncle Lance!" Dylan held up the sled.

"Go," Erin said. "The boys have been really excited about today. I've been promising them for weeks that as soon as we got a good snow, we'd go sledding."

And every day since her accident, she'd put them off. Or rather, he'd put them off. As he jogged over to the boys, he realized he'd been working hard at keeping his distance, trying not to let how they had so easily taken to calling him "Uncle Lance" or how they automatically included him in everything, be caught in his heart.

Was there a way for him to maintain a relationship with them once he left? He took the sled from Dylan and carried it the rest of the way up the hill. It wasn't much of a hill, just a gentle, sloping space that would allow the boys the enjoyment of sledding but not the high-speed thrills he and Erin used to chase after.

They'd had a lot of fun together. Funny how it had taken being apart almost two years to remember it.

The boys got on the sled and Lance gave them a small push to send them sailing down the hill. He ran after them, letting their laughter warm his heart.

It was going to be impossible not to find himself attached. It hadn't hurt as much leaving the boys behind the first time; he'd been too deep in his own grief to understand how big a part of his life they were.

When they reached the bottom of the hill, the edge of the sled hit a tiny bump and sent the boys flying. Even though they were laughing, Lance ran over to make sure they were okay.

"Again!" Ryan chortled, jumping up and running toward him.

Dylan picked up the sled and followed his brother.

"That was awesome. We probably flew a hundred feet in the air."

They hadn't flown at all, but the boys' excitement made him smile. After losing Lily and Erin, Lance had vowed not to remarry or have children. He'd jokingly told people that he was married to his company and that it was enough. But as the snowy boys rushed at him with open arms, he thought that perhaps he might have been too hasty. He found his work rewarding, but no one from the office ever ran around giving him hugs. Not only would it be inappropriate, as much as he liked the people he worked with, he hadn't ever felt like hugging any of them.

He looked up from the boys and over at Erin as she watched. She set the camera down and waved at him. Lance waved back, feeling like a schoolboy as he noticed her shining eyes. She might not have been able to join in on the fun, but she was clearly enjoying herself.

"Come on, Uncle Lance." Dylan tugged on his pants, so he grabbed the sled and they made the trek back up the hill. He used to laugh at all the people who talked about living for the moment; he'd never understood why they weren't planning for their futures. But now he almost understood. He should have kept his distance, knowing that the inevitable goodbye was coming. As he got the boys situated on the sled for another trip down the hill, he pushed aside his worries for the future and sent the boys sailing again.

Maybe he'd lost his chance to be a dad, and he wouldn't remain an uncle much longer, but for now it was enough. He'd find a way to deal with the inevitable pain later.

* * *

Even though Erin hadn't been able to do any sledding, she'd had enough fun just watching everyone. It had been a long time since she'd seen Lance let loose like that. Everything since Lily had been born was about being responsible and doing the right thing. It was funny how he liked to mock her lists, but he had a similar need for organization and control.

When they'd met, Lance had been one of the most fun people she'd ever been around besides her sisters. They used to have wild adventures together—not the crazy college-party thing, but things like hiking and camping or sledding. She didn't think Lance had been sledding since before Lily was born. He hadn't wanted to go without her and he'd always been so busy at work. He used to tell her that he was working hard for Lily's future. But what good was the future if you didn't take the time to enjoy the present? Did he regret all the time he'd spent at work instead of with their family?

The sun was getting low in the sky, which meant they only had a little bit of daylight left to feed the horses and take care of the other chores. Shane had brought his horses over while they were on their honeymoon so Erin wouldn't have to go back and forth. At the time she'd thought it was a needless effort. But now she was glad.

"Time to come in," she called when Lance and the boys got to the bottom of the hill for what had to be the thousandth time.

They came to her, disappointment overshadowing their laughter.

"Do you think we can do it again tomorrow?" Dylan asked.

"We'll see," she said. "Right now, we need to feed the animals."

The trouble with having broken limbs was that the animals didn't know any differently. They still had to be cared for. One more thing Erin had to give credit to Lance for. Despite his lack of experience, he'd still jumped in to do everything that was needed. The boys ran past her to the barn, already knowing their jobs. They would get out the hose and refill the water while Lance took care of the hay.

Lance stayed behind, walking alongside her. "You're not too tired, are you? I didn't mean for us to stay out so long. I can't remember when I've had so much fun."

She turned and smiled at him. "I'm glad. I was just thinking that it must've been a long time since you've been sledding."

He nodded slowly. "Not since that last time before Lily was born."

He stopped, holding her back slightly. "What went wrong with us? I keep thinking about that day and how much in love we were, and I don't understand how we lost it so easily. What happened to all those plans of forever?"

A lot of things. But when she'd pointed them out to him in counseling, he'd bristled, telling her it wasn't fair to blame him for her decision to leave. When she'd pushed too hard, he'd ended the conversation. So what could she say now? He'd come here, looking for peace after their divorce. Even though she had her own part in their relationship breakdown, she knew that until he accepted what he'd done wrong in the marriage, he wouldn't be able to find that peace.

"Sometimes having fun and being in love isn't enough to make a marriage work," she said finally.

He gave her the same confused look he'd given her when she'd asked for the divorce. "Then what? What else does a marriage need?"

The boys couldn't be left unattended in the barn for too long. Nicole's horse, Snookie, while much better trained than she'd been when they'd first gotten her, was still uncomfortable around children. The boys knew not to go near her, but that didn't mean they always listened.

Erin took another step toward the barn. "Every marriage is different. And I know, after everything you've done to help me the past few days, I owe you a better explanation. But I need to make sure the boys are safe. So I'll tell you what. One of these nights, when the boys are in bed, you and I can have some hot chocolate and we'll talk. I may not totally have the answers you're looking for, but I can at least tell you what else I needed, if that's something you're open to hearing."

He started for the barn. "You're right. I wasn't even thinking about the boys."

He shook his head slowly then stopped again. "This is why I don't do emotions. You used to always get on me about that, wanting to know how I felt. But here I am, feeling things I don't understand, and I've already lost sight of what's important." Not waiting for an answer, he continued toward the barn.

If she could sum up precisely why she'd finally decided that their marriage couldn't be saved, his previous words would do that nicely. He thought emotions got in the way of more important business. But, for her, emotions *were* important business. And when you didn't deal with them, they clogged up everything else. Though he was quick to dismiss those feelings, she didn't think they were gone at all. They might not be front and center, but they were there, lurking. Even though Lance hadn't yet told her exactly what he'd meant by making peace with her, she suspected that his lack of peace stemmed from having dismissed all his emotions.

She let him go on ahead, giving him space to sort out whatever was in his head as she came up slowly behind him. Lance had fed the horses enough times that he knew what to do and how much.

Maybe someday they'd come to a place of enough understanding that they could have this conversation and it would not be so difficult for Lance. But that was on him to figure out. Her divorce had taught her that it wasn't her job to fix Lance. He had to choose for himself what was important to him and why.

When she got to the barn, she didn't see Lance or the boys near the horses, but she could hear them in the tack room. Hopefully, Dylan wasn't trying to talk him into some of his shenanigans. Though Shane had firmly told the boys they couldn't go riding until he was home, Dylan had mentioned almost every day that he wanted to go riding.

"What's going on?" she asked when she entered the room.

The boys looked like they were about to cry. Lance didn't look like he was faring much better.

"Fluffy the Second didn't eat her breakfast," Dylan said.

Fluffy the Second was the barn cat they'd gotten a few weeks ago from Ricky. Their last barn cat had disappeared a couple of months ago and the boys had been devastated. Unfortunately a ranch was a dangerous place for barn cats, with all the predators wandering around. Hence, Fluffy's status of being the second and the boys' concern over the untouched bowl of cat food.

"Maybe she went to visit a friend," Erin suggested.

Dylan looked at her like she was an idiot. "Cats don't have friends. My friend Jake said that Fluffy the First probably got eaten by a coyote."

Ryan started to cry. And poor Lance looked like he wanted to do about the same. Lance's discomfort with emotion also meant that he couldn't stand watching anyone cry. Erin knew from experience that he would do just about anything to keep a child from crying.

"I'm sure Jake doesn't know everything about cats," Lance said. "Weren't you just telling me that Snookie is Elmer's girlfriend? If a horse can have a girlfriend, why can't a cat have a regular friend?"

Dylan looked thoughtful for a moment. "Because when Fluffy the First went missing, Mom said the same thing. But I overheard Dad telling Uncle Fernando that one of the critters probably got him. That means a coyote."

As he spoke, Erin was frantically gesturing to get him to stop. His words only made Ryan cry harder. Ryan's poor little heart was breaking at the thought of losing another cat. She went over to the bench and held her arms out to Ryan, who climbed onto her lap, sobbing against her chest. Erin rubbed his back as she glared at Dylan.

"What?" Dylan asked. "I'm only telling the truth. When you're a cowboy, living on a ranch, you have to know the facts of life."

The little boy's seriousness made Erin want to laugh. But Ryan was still so upset, she didn't dare. Besides, Dylan needed to learn a little sensitivity when it came to sharing those facts.

"One bowl of uneaten food does not mean we lost Fluffy the Second to a coyote," Erin said firmly. She cuddled Ryan closer to her and gave him a kiss on top of his head. "I'm sure she's fine. But we can say a prayer for her, just in case."

She glanced up at Lance, who had turned white. She'd already overloaded him emotionally and this had probably taken him over the top. Helping Erin had probably turned into way more than Lance had bargained for, poor guy.

Her suggestion caused Ryan to stop sniffling and look up.

"But what if it doesn't work, like when we prayed for Fluffy the First?"

One more parent thing she hadn't been prepared to deal with. But she could feel Lance's expectant gaze upon her. A man who'd lost his faith and two little boys who were just developing theirs needed to hear some kind of wisdom about what it meant to pray for their lost cat.

Lance had ridiculed her for her faith when they'd lost Lily. She never could explain to him why, just that she still trusted in God's goodness. That was how she felt about the missing cat.

Would God bring Fluffy the Second back to them safely?

She had no idea. But she had to trust in God's answer.

"Prayer doesn't change God's mind," she said finally. “But sharing our thoughts with Him brings Him closer to us. He can give us love and comfort in this time, and remembering how He’s comforted us now, we can look back on it in the future, knowing that whatever comes our way, God will be there for us.”

Three blank stares weighed heavily on her. “When you tell your friends about your problems, do your friends ever fix them?” she asked.

She looked over at Dylan. “When you told Jake about Fluffy the First, did it change the result of what happened to him?”

Dylan shook his head.

“But did you feel better?” she asked.

“Yes,” Dylan said, nodding slowly. “I knew he understood how I felt because a coyote ate one of his cats.”

She squeezed her eyes shut and prayed for patience. They needed to get off the cat-eating coyote subject. But at least he’d proved her point.

“And that’s what prayer is. We’re sharing the deepest parts of our hearts with God because we know He understands. He might not change the circumstances, but at least we know He’s there for us and wants to show His love for us.”

Ryan wiped his nose on his sleeve and looked up at her. “But I want Fluffy the Second back.”

She didn’t know how else to help a four-year-old understand.

“We all do. But you know how sometimes you ask your mom for a cookie and she says yes, but sometimes she says no? You know your mom still loves you even if you can’t have another cookie. That’s how God is,” she said, hoping she'd gotten a little closer with her description.

Ryan rested his head on her chest. "Mom only lets me have cookies sometimes and she says too many cookies are bad for me."

Dylan came and put his arm around her. "I snuck some cookies one time after mom said no. I ate them all. But then I had a stomachache and I threw up."

One more illustration she wasn't going for.

Ryan gave another big sniffle, wiped his nose again and looked at his brother. "That's why you should listen to Mom even if you don't like it."

Then Dylan turned his attention to her. "So it's kind of like that with God? You can ask Him for stuff but He might still say no."

"It's exactly like that," she said.

The boys exchanged the kind of look Erin and her sisters used to share with one another, a secret language only they understood. Whatever the boys were communicating, it gave Erin confidence that they at least had figured it out among themselves.

Ryan climbed off her lap and started back toward the main barn. "Maybe tomorrow we can go look for Fluffy the Second."

"That sounds like a great plan," Erin said. Hopefully they'd find the cat safe and sound. "In the meantime, do you want to say a prayer for Fluffy the Second?"

Dylan stood tall. "Can I say the prayer?"

It was tempting to say no. Who knew what would come out of the little boy's mouth next? But how could she deny the faith of a child?

"Sure, go ahead."

Dylan clasped his hands together and above his

head. "Dear God, please bring Fluffy the Second back home safely. And if a coyote has eaten her, please give him a really bad tummy ache so he never eats anyone else's cats again. Amen."

Lance gave a kind of chortle snort, like he was desperately trying not to laugh and having difficulty keeping it in. And as much as Erin would have preferred a more proper prayer, she knew it came from the heart and couldn't fault Dylan for his honesty.

"Amen," Erin said, smiling at the little boy. "Now let's get the other animals fed."

The boys ran out of the tack room, but Lance paused beside her. "Do you really believe all that stuff?"

She nodded. "I think that's one of the problems between you and me. I do believe it. I can't pretend to understand why God allows bad things to happen, but I can choose to believe in God's goodness. And that even though I don't always get the outcome I would like, He still hears my prayers and holds me close to Him, even when my heart is breaking."

"I don't know if I believe that," Lance said.

Erin stood and reached out to give him a little squeeze. "I know. And I hope you know that regardless of whether or not you believe in Him, He believes in you. God loves you, and I hope that someday you're able to recognize that."

Lance gave a jerky nod to indicate having heard her and then turned and left the tack room.

Piling on the emotion and then telling him about God was probably more than he could handle. But that was the thing about life. It often gave you more than you thought you could handle. For Erin the solution was to press on and try to make the best of it. But Lance had run from it and buried himself in his work. She'd always resented his work and even though she'd known that some of it was because work provided a convenient excuse to avoid emotions, she also had to recognize that in some ways, work provided him with comfort. Maybe it was a false comfort, but it was comfort nonetheless. Maybe, as much as she'd been judging him and wanting him to understand her, she should have also spent time trying to understand him.

As she followed him into the main barn, her heart felt heavier knowing that she held a slightly higher level of blame than she'd been giving herself for the breakdown of her marriage. Not that it was about blame but about realizing it wasn't just Lance's heart that needed some repair work, but her own.

Chapter Four

Though Lance was trying to treat Erin's Christmas planner as a simple to-do list, he hadn't counted on how it would tear him apart inside. He'd been hanging decorations and finishing the lights, and all of it was way too much, in his opinion. But he wasn't about to let Erin do it herself, which she threatened to do every time he questioned her. Of course, there was that box of mistletoe he'd made mysteriously disappear. There were some things Lance wasn't going to do, even if it was in the name of making peace for the sake of getting back to business.

That was why he was grateful to arrive at Sunday. All he had to do was to drop Erin and the kids off at church and then go to the café to relax for a while, maybe explore the town, then go and pick Erin and the kids up.

It wasn't so much that he minded helping her. But things were starting to get intense—too intense—and he wasn't sure how to deal with it all. Erin said to take it to God. But God hadn't done him any favors and he couldn't imagine Him doing so now.

He'd talked to his counselor a couple of times on the phone. When he'd called to reschedule his sessions due to helping Erin, his counselor had told him they could do his sessions remotely if he wanted. So far, his phone calls with his counselor hadn't gotten him any answers, because she'd just told him to think about what it all meant and that he was on the right track. Wasn't that her job? To tell him what it meant?

Maybe, alone in the café, he'd have enough space from Erin and the boys to find the answers for himself.

When they got to the church, the place looked like one of those picture-book churches. All white, with a steeple, and decorated with more lights and other holiday accoutrements than Lance could remember seeing in one place. Except, of course, for Erin's holiday horror show.

"It's cute, isn't it?" Erin said as he pulled to a stop.

"That's a lot of lights," he said. "You must've had a hand in those decorations."

She laughed. "I am on the decorating committee, but none of this was my idea. Every year, they have a light show timed to music that brings in people from all over the area to enjoy the holiday spirit. On some evenings, they can come in for a cookie and warm beverage."

Lance shook his head. "And then I'm sure you tell them all about how wonderful your church is and how they need to come to Jesus."

"No," Erin said, sounding offended. "I mean, yes, we'd love for the people to come to our church and start attending, but that's not why we do it. The surrounding ranch community is so large that we often don't have the opportunity to see one another and many people don't have a safe social outlet. So this is just a place for them to come and enjoy the holiday spirit. Mrs. Davis, who organizes the event, stopped coming to church years ago. The point isn't to force anyone to believe in God, because that's up to the individual to choose. But we would like to think that regardless of whether or not you go to our church, or even believe in God, you find a welcome here."

It sounded like a nice enough place. If you were into all that holiday cheer, which, obviously, Lance wasn't. He had enough holiday nonsense to last him a lifetime.

When Erin and the kids got out of the car and went into the church, he saw people come around them, greeting them warmly, like she was a long-lost friend they hadn't seen in years, even though it had only been two weeks.

Maybe this wasn't the place for him, but it warmed his heart to see Erin accepted into a community that she clearly loved as much as they loved her. They'd tried going to a couple of churches while they were married, but so many of them were filled with snooty ladies that Erin never connected with, and even though Erin had always said she had a deep faith in God, sometimes it was just easier to not bother with going to church.

But at the warm welcome she'd just received, Lance could understand why this place was important to her. In some ways he kind of envied that.

He headed down the street to the café Erin had pointed out when they'd driven into town. She'd told him that the bear claws were delicious and the coffee was as good as anything you could get in the city.

The parking lot next to the café was surprisingly

empty, but then he thought about how full the church parking lot was and figured they all must be there.

When he entered, the place looked just like the kind of quaint coffee shop he'd expect in a small town. One of the corners had a sign designating it the Kiddie Corral and he could see it had an assortment of toys, games and small tables. He walked up to the counter, where an older woman turned and greeted him warmly. "Welcome. It's cold out there. What can I get to warm you up?"

She didn't wear a name tag, but he could tell by her attitude that she must be Della, the owner Erin had told him about. "I'd like a large coffee, black, and one of your famous bear claws. I've been told not to miss them."

Della beamed proudly. "And just who told you that?"

"Erin Drummond," he said. "I'm helping her out while her sisters are out of town."

Della's eyes widened. "O-oh, a boyfriend? I knew Erin wouldn't stay single for long. She's one of those women with a heart of gold. But I don't have to tell you about it. You probably already know."

Erin had mentioned not giving up on love, but it was weird hearing it from someone else. "Not a boyfriend," he said. Even though it was technically correct to say he was her ex-husband, it didn't feel right to do so in front of a woman who clearly thought the world of Erin. "Just an old friend."

Della's eyes gleamed. "But you want to be. I can pick them out every time. I keep thinking I should run a service. You know those people who come here when they go on dates from those online matchmaking services? I can usually tell within five minutes if things are going to work out for them. If they would just consult with me, I could save them a whole lot of heartache. And you, young man, have the look of someone who would give Erin forever."

Wow, was that a lot to be thrown at you at once. He hadn't been called young man in a long time, but he knew Della didn't mean it offensively. She just saw him as someone with his whole life ahead of him, a future to be had, and she didn't know what he'd gone through already. If she had known, she'd have probably changed her description to his being an old man. As for forever with Erin, he'd tried that and she'd walked away.

"I think you're mistaken," he said. "I was just passing through on business, and Erin fell, breaking her arm and her ankle. The doctor didn't think she should be home alone with the boys. I have some time off, so I thought I'd stick around to help out. That way her sisters didn't have to come home from their honeymoons early."

He didn't know why he was telling this woman so much, but as supportive as she sounded, he couldn't help himself.

A puzzled look crossed her face. "Erin got hurt? Well, I guess that's why I haven't seen her in here lately. I just assumed she's been busy chasing those little terrors around and getting ready for Christmas."

The boys might not be his, but something about having them referred to as "little terrors" rankled.

"They're very good boys, they just have a lot of energy."

He gave her a firm look, which he'd been told scared most people.

But Della appeared unaffected. "The little one is

an absolute delight. But that Dylan? I can't tell you all the shenanigans he and my grandson get into. It's all good-natured fun. But when you say they have a lot of energy, you aren't kidding. They had a play date at my house once, and I've never been so exhausted. That's why the Good Lord makes it so you can't have children after a certain age. You're just too tired to chase them around."

The warmth in her voice made him realize that she, too, cared for the boys. He didn't know why it affected him so profoundly, but it felt good to know that the boys and Erin had a group of people surrounding them with so much love. It wasn't his place to be concerned, but he couldn't help doing so anyway.

That brought up more of the emotion he was trying to avoid. He was leaving in a week. And who knew if he'd be able to see the boys again?

Della handed him a steaming mug of coffee and a plate with the bear claw on it. "I hope it's as good as Erin has been claiming. Wouldn't want anyone to be disappointed."

He took a sip of the coffee and savored it. "If the bear claw is half as good as this coffee, then you have nothing to worry about."

"It's just coffee," Della said. "A monkey could make it."

Lance grinned. "Then a monkey can cook better than I can."

"Now you're just being sweet. You turn on that charm for Erin and I guarantee we'll be hearing wedding bells by summer. It's a shame that fool she used to be married to couldn't see it."

He was suddenly glad he hadn't introduced himself as her ex. Della would probably have put arsenic in his coffee. Besides, he hadn't divorced Erin. She'd divorced him. And, not to contradict the expert, but whatever charms Della thought he had, Erin had clearly disagreed.

"Well, like I said, we're just friends. I'm going to go sit over by that nice fireplace and do some work on my computer while I wait for Erin to get out of church."

"You want me to turn the fireplace on for you?" Della asked. "We can't have a real fire due to fire code, but I think it adds a nice touch. I just don't like having a fire for only me."

"That would be great, thanks. I've enjoyed the fires at Erin's. It makes the place so cozy."

As much as he'd thought the way his house was decorated was just fine, and even though he'd somewhat mocked Erin's décor, being back in her space kind of made him a little regretful he'd let their house get so impersonal. But maybe, once he got home, he could change that. He'd definitely forgo all the Christmas decorations, but he'd taken a liking to the soft throw blankets and he would definitely look into getting a cute electric fireplace like Della's.

Della came over and turned on the fireplace. "Why aren't you at church with Erin?"

Exactly the reason he hadn't wanted to go in and meet her friends. He hadn't wanted to answer the questions and he hadn't wanted them trying to tell him why he should give their church a try. As it was, sitting here in the empty coffee shop with Della, he was starting to feel a little uncomfortable about the fact that she clearly knew a lot about him. She was the type of person who wouldn't be satisfied with a polite answer.

"Church isn't my thing," he said, hoping it would be enough to get her to understand that he didn't want to talk about it.

For a moment Della looked like she was going to say something, but then she shrugged. "I suppose you've got your reasons. Not my job to judge. I just know that life is better with the Good Lord in your back pocket."

In your back pocket? That seemed like an odd way to describe it.

He looked up at her. "How do you know you've got Him? And how do you know He's good?"

Della pointed to his as of yet untouched bear claw. "You eat. I need to know if my baking is as good as Erin has been telling people."

He took a bite and Erin's recommendation did not disappoint.

At his smile, Della nodded approvingly. "You took it on faith that my bear claw was good. And that's how you have to take God, too."

He braced himself for a sermon, but she turned and walked away. So he continued munching on his pastry and booted up his computer.

Watching the emails filter in didn't make him feel any better about the time he'd been forced to take off. In fact, it was depressing to see how little they needed him. He'd been copied on a lot of emails, but in terms of him needing to act on anything, there was nothing. Granted, everyone knew he was taking a leave of absence, but it put a sick feeling in the pit of his stomach to know that for all of the time he'd invested in his company, when it came to all the reasons he thought he was supposed to be there, it didn't seem like any of them were true.

Chad had even let the controller go, at least, according to this email. Wait. What? Janelle was good at her job and had saved the company millions of dollars. Why would Chad let her go without even talking to Lance?

Lance pulled out his phone and texted Chad. Chad wasn't the churchgoing type, either, and he spent just as many hours at the office as Lance did. A few seconds later, he got a text back.

Long story. I'm handling it. You focus on getting better.

How was he supposed to focus on getting better when the only thing that ever kept him sane was his work and now he was finding out just how irrelevant he was in it?

Fortunately he was still the only person in the coffee shop and Della had gone into the back. He hit the button for Chad's cell.

"I said I'm handling it," Chad said without greeting him.

"I still own fifty percent of the company," Lance said. "Or are you going back on your word and finding someone to buy my shares and force me out?"

"I would never do that to you," Chad said quietly. "I meant what I said when I told you that you needed a break to deal with your divorce and Lily's death. I just got a report from the counselor, who said you're making progress. I don't know what that means, and I know you don't like to talk about it, but you know I'm not just your partner, but your friend."

When Chad had come to him with the ultimatum that he get help or he'd bring in an investor to force

Lance out, he claimed he was doing it as a friend. At the time, Lance had thought he was just paying lip service to the word. But he could hear genuine compassion in Chad's voice.

At least Lance's counselor was giving Chad answers. But being told he was making progress was a lot different than being told he was better and could return to work.

Still, Chad was right. Whatever Erin thought of Chad, Chad was Lance's friend.

"I'm at Erin's," Lance said.

Chad didn't answer at first and Lance hadn't expected him to. He wasn't even sure why he'd led with that fact.

"Are you two getting back together?"

He should have given more information. "No. As part of my therapy, I'm supposed to make peace with her. I don't know what it means… But Erin was in an accident and she needed my help. So I'm here, helping Erin and trying to figure out—"

What was he trying to figure out? So far, he wasn't doing much figuring, just checking off items on Erin's list. And trying not to think about the emotions being with her and the boys was stirring up.

Was that what making peace meant?

Or was it as his counselor had said, that he needed to deal with those emotions? He was trying not to, especially because all it would mean was Erin telling him "I told you so."

What mattered to him more? Being back in on the daily operations of his business and feeling like he mattered again? Or not having to hear Erin triumph over him?

"That's good of you," Chad said. "I don't know a lot of guys who would help their ex out, especially after what she did to you."

His first thought was to defend Erin. He had to admit, after spending this time with her, she wasn't the heartless woman he'd been painting her as. She was hurting, too, and he'd been too busy fighting with her to see that.

As weird as that thought was, something about it felt good. Even though he still couldn't define what his counselor had meant by making peace with Erin, this made him feel like he was closer to that goal.

"It's more complicated than that, but I will say that I feel better about everything that happened."

He hadn't voiced that thought before and while he still couldn't say he forgave her, he also couldn't say he hated her anymore, either.

But that wasn't what this call was about. "Look, I know you're worried about me, but the biggest thing I've realized in being away is how much I love what we do. It's an important part of my life and I don't think you understand how hard it has been to walk away. So tell me, what's going on with Janelle?"

The long pause on the line made him wonder if Chad was going to answer his question. Then Chad said, "We think she's been embezzling from us."

Janelle? Embezzling? That didn't sound like the woman he'd known for years.

"How do you know? What would make you even suspect her?"

Even though Chad should have anticipated these questions, he took even longer to answer.

"I hired a firm to go through our books."

There was something in Chad's voice that made Lance realize his friend wasn't telling him everything.

"You were trying to get a business valuation to force me out, weren't you?"

"I can't run this business on my own. And you were in the middle of a weird breakdown that made me think I couldn't count on you anymore. Most people would've just forced you out. But, man, we built this thing together. I'd like to think that loyalty still has value in this world. Just because I got the valuation doesn't mean I'm going to use it."

It made good business sense, figuring out what the company was worth. What his share was worth. But it still hurt that Chad had gone behind his back to do it.

"So what now?" Lance's voice cracked as he asked the question, and it hurt just as much as it had when he'd asked a similar question of Erin. He closed his eyes and braced himself for the "I'm sorry" that was likely coming.

"How long are you stuck with Erin?"

"Her sisters are due back in less than a week. Once they get here, she won't need me anymore."

The long pause gave Lance hope that maybe this wasn't the end.

"I'll send you what I have on Janelle. Take a look and see why I let her go. And I'll send you the résumés I've been reviewing. You can give me some feedback."

He wasn't back in, but he wasn't out, either. He hoped he could prove to Chad that he was still capable of being an active partner in their business.

"Sounds good. I'm assuming I still have access to all the files?"

"You'll need a new password, because we changed

everything when Janelle left. I'll have IT contact you first thing tomorrow to get you set up."

That would be the test then. If Lance actually could access everything, then he knew Chad still had a little faith in him.

"Thanks. Stay in touch, will you? I haven't liked not being part of the business, and the fact that so much has changed already tells me I can't keep my finger off the pulse of things for very long. Our company is important to me. I wouldn't be here with Erin otherwise."

He took another sip of his coffee, hoping his words would sink in.

Then Chad said, "I didn't think of it that way. You must want back in pretty badly to make such a sacrifice. When you're done with her, come see me and we'll talk."

As Lance hung up the phone, he felt bad that he'd let Chad think his being there was a sacrifice. It was hard, yes, but he'd have to admit that he'd been enjoying it. He'd forgotten how much fun he and Erin had together and even though things were strained between them at times, he was also remembering how much he genuinely liked her as a person. Maybe they were just one of those couples who, while they couldn't make it work romantically, were better off as friends.

Could being Erin's friend be what making peace with her meant?

His alarm went off, indicating it was time to pick up Erin and the boys. As he packed up his laptop, Della came out of the back, carrying a small box.

"I didn't want to interrupt, because it sounded like an important phone call, but I wanted to send a little something for Erin and the boys. Their mother doesn't let them have sweets very often, but with her out of town, I figure what she doesn't know won't hurt her. Besides, I owe Erin a thank-you for saying such nice things about my bear claws."

The woman's kindness touched him and he could see why this place meant so much to Erin.

"Thank you," he said. "She's told me how much she loves this town, and if the rest of the people here are as kind as you, I can see why."

As Della handed him the box, she gave him a small squeeze.

"It's hard to have faith when it seems like life is beating you up. But it's the only way I know how to get through any of it. That, and surrounding yourself with people who will love and support you. Erin is a good woman. It's obvious you care about her. So don't give up on her."

He didn't have any plans to stick around past the arrival of Erin's sisters, and he likely wouldn't have the opportunity to come here again. Even though Della's advice was completely misguided, it meant a lot that she saw something in him and chose to reach out.

"Thank you," he said. "I appreciate it, but there won't be wedding bells again for Erin and me. I'm her ex-husband. I didn't give up on her. She left me."

He turned and left, not wanting to further his discussion with Della but also not wanting to leave Erin waiting. She still had a ways to go in her recovery and she still often got tired if she was on her feet for too long.

That, and he didn't want Della to come back with any kind of encouragement that there was hope for the two of them. He didn't think his heart could take being torn apart anymore. He was barely clinging to the only thing he had left of value in his life—his business—so to think that anything else was possible was too much.

Chapter Five

Lance seemed different when he came to pick Erin and the kids up from church. Erin wanted to speak up, to ask him about it, but she didn't know how he would take it.

Ricky had taken her to task at church for not bringing Lance by. He'd insisted that she invite Lance to his Christmas gathering tomorrow at the Double R. But it was awkward, showing your ex-husband around and introducing him. It was hard enough at church, answering everyone's questions about this Uncle Lance the boys talked about nonstop.

She was glad the boys had taken to Lance, but it also made it difficult, explaining their complicated relationship. Worse, it was clear to her that the boys had already become attached to him. What would it look like when her sisters came back and Lance left? Would Lance want to visit them again? Would it be uncomfortable as they both moved on with their lives, possibly meeting someone new?

Erin had to laugh at that thought. As much as she

said she was open to dating again, there weren't a lot of single men her age around town.

And, if she were honest, there weren't a lot of men out there who could measure up to the standard Lance had set. His giving heart, especially in light of the fact that she was his ex-wife and he was doing so much to help her, was something she hadn't seen in others. If only he wasn't so emotionally unavailable.

"I went to the café," he said. "Della sent me home with a box of goodies for you guys."

"Thanks," Erin said, taking the box. She looked down at it then over at her group of friends gathering near the church steps to go out to lunch. She and the boys usually joined them, but it felt too awkward to ask. It was going to be hard enough passing on Ricky's invitation.

Erin took a deep breath. "Ricky is having some people over for sleigh rides tomorrow to celebrate the start of winter break. If it's not too much trouble, I'd love for you to take us."

"Ricky," Lance muttered. "Always Ricky."

Was he jealous of Ricky? Lance had never been the type to get jealous. But it would explain why he'd give her such a non-answer to a basic question.

"You know Ricky is my boss, right? You have nothing to worry about."

Lance looked over at her. "It wouldn't be the first time a woman dated her boss."

So he *was* jealous. Erin let out a long sigh. "He's in his eighties. His wife died years ago and he's been a confirmed bachelor ever since. You might hear him jokingly flirt with women from time to time, but he buried his heart with his late wife."

"It's none of my business," Lance said.

"It's not, but you get angry whenever his name comes up. I thought if I explained, you'd feel better about the situation. So why don't we go for the sleigh ride and you can see for yourself that he's not a threat."

"I have no reason to be threatened by him."

As she glanced at him she could see that he was gripping the steering wheel so tightly his knuckles were turning white.

She touched his arm. "You're right, you don't. I know you think I've done a lot of things to hurt you, but I would never flaunt someone I'm dating in front of you. If there was a special someone in my life, he would be here helping me."

He glanced at her and she could see the pain in his eyes. Why couldn't he just tell her how he felt about things? And why couldn't she find a man who was as caring as Lance but also able to express those emotions?

"Uncle Lance?" Dylan's voice rang out from the backseat. "Mr. Ricky is a real nice man. Sometimes he lets us ride his horses. Not all of them, because some of them are very expensive."

Erin smiled at the way her nephew emphasized the words "very expensive." Ricky was always going on about how expensive his horses were and it was funny how the boys had picked up on that. But it wasn't surprising. They were smart kids.

"You'd like him," Dylan continued. "He's a real cowboy. He might teach you, just like my dad is teaching me. Please, will you let us go for the sleigh ride? If you've never been on a sleigh ride, it's not at all scary."

She shouldn't have asked Lance in front of the boys.

It didn't seem right to get their hopes up and she certainly didn't want to make Lance out to be the bad guy for saying no.

"We'll have to take a look at your aunt's list and see if we could fit it in," Lance said. At least he'd found a way to give himself an out. It would be a shame to miss the sleigh ride, but Lance had already sacrificed so much for her, she wasn't going to ask him to do more, even if his reasons for being uncomfortable were silly.

"Great idea," Erin quickly added. "I didn't even think to check the calendar. We might have something else going on."

The only thing on the calendar was the sleigh ride, but if Lance didn't want to go, she'd let him take the out. The boys hadn't seen the calendar, so they wouldn't know any differently. Hopefully, though, she could convince him. The sleigh ride was one of the few things she could do with her injuries, and it had been a lot of fun last year when Ricky had done it for Christmas. Ricky was getting older and even though they would all like to think he'd be around forever, Erin knew better than anyone how quickly that could change.

"I want to go to Ricky's," Ryan said. The whine was mostly that of a cranky four-year-old who'd probably had too much sugar in Sunday school. It seemed like this time of year all the teachers were bringing in some kind of treat for the children.

Erin turned and smiled at her nephew. "I told you, we would check the calendar."

The boys looked disappointed but they also knew that if they persisted, they would not get to go at all. When they got home the boys ran inside, but Lance stopped her. “It’s not that big of a deal. We can go if you want. I’m not jealous.”

The way he kept denying it was kind of sweet. But it also made her want to analyze her own feelings. What would she do if Lance had a girlfriend?

The answer created an uneasy feeling in her stomach.

“It isn’t about you being jealous. I’m just trying to be considerate of your feelings, and you don’t sound very interested in going to the Double R. You sacrificed so much for me, being here this week, and I want to make sure we’re not imposing on you too much.”

He looked uncomfortable, like he didn’t want her thanks, nor did he want to talk about any of this. Part of why even trying to have a relationship with him was so difficult sometimes.

“It’s not an imposition. I’m happy to help. Like I said when I came here, I needed to make peace with you. I guess this is how I’m doing it.”

If his words weren’t so stilted, she might have believed him. But he sounded so weird about everything, and so unlike himself, she knew there was more to it. A gust of wind came upon them, making her shiver.

“Let’s get you inside where it’s warm,” he said. “The last thing I need is for you to get a cold.”

He helped her into the house, even though she didn’t much need assistance to get around anymore. She’d gotten pretty good at maneuvering in her walking boot, which made her feel like less of a burden on Lance. But he still automatically reached for her arm to help her. And even though she probably shouldn’t like it so much, it felt good, the gentle way he cared for her.

She followed him inside, where the boys were already engrossed in the train set. They'd always loved their trains, but at Christmas, Erin turned their little train set into part of the holiday décor. They even had special holiday buildings for the boys' train town. Granted they were pieces that probably belonged in one of those Christmas villages people liked to set up, but Erin and her sisters had never seen the point in decorations the children could look at but not touch. In a home with small children, breakage was bound to happen, so they always focused on having things they didn't need to worry about.

"Uncle Lance! Play trains with us!" Ryan ran up to them, holding his favorite engine. He'd been giving Lance the honor of playing with the treasured toy a lot the past couple of days, and though Lance probably didn't understand the significance, Erin did.

The boys loved their uncle Lance, even though he wasn't exactly their uncle anymore. So how did she make a difficult adult situation fair for two little boys who had nothing to do with it?

Lance patted his laptop bag. "When I was at the café, I talked to my partner, who needed me to do some work for him. I'm going to go set up in the kitchen and take care of it."

She should have known it was too good to be true that he would spend all this time here and not work. She'd seen him on his laptop a few times, but this was the first he'd brushed off the boys. He didn't owe her anything. He was just there to be a responsible adult in case there was something she couldn't do.

A puzzled look crossed Ryan's face. Lance hadn't told him no before. "Will you play with me when you're done?"

Did Lance remember these conversations back when they were married? How many times Dylan had come to him, wanting to play, but Lance'd had work to do? They'd had the same experience with Ryan and Lily, but it had been a little different since the two of them had been so much younger. But Dylan? He was watching for Lance's current response. Maybe he didn't have an exact memory of that time, but there was something inside him that probably remembered all the times Lance had said "later," only "later" never came.

"Let me just review these files and then I'll be there," Lance said.

Good old Lance. It seemed like every time her heart softened toward him just a little more, and she wanted to reach out to him to see if maybe there was something worth salvaging in their relationship, he'd say or do something to remind her exactly why it hadn't worked the first time.

Dylan came up to his brother and put his arm around him. "It's okay. We don't need Uncle Lance. You can use my new tanker if you want."

Even though it warmed her heart to see Dylan act so lovingly toward his brother, it also broke Erin's heart just a little. She could remember growing up with her sisters how many times she and Leah would step in to do something kind for Nicole because their father had rejected her once again. At least Dylan and Ryan had a father now who would never make them feel rejected like that. It was just a shame they'd already learned the behavior to make up for it.

As the boys ran back into the other room, Lance turned and looked at her. "I know the disapproving look on your face. Can't you give me a break once in a while?"

One more thing that only made her feel sad about the relationship. He could tell when she was disappointed and his response was to be defensive about it. And she hadn't said a word.

"I didn't say anything. It's been good of you to be here all week without needing to work. I would never ask you to sacrifice your job for me. I tried that once and it didn't work out so well."

She probably shouldn't have even said that much, because the anger that flashed across Lance's face told her that they were back in their old familiar cycle of arguing about priorities.

She gave him a small smile. "I didn't mean to criticize you. I'm sorry. I'm sure I sounded ungrateful, when I can't tell you how much I appreciate you being here. You get your computer set up and I'll heat you up some hot chocolate and see what kind of treats Della sent."

The relief on his face told her that she'd managed to defuse the situation. But it kind of made her heart hurt, just a little. If she were honest with herself, she'd admit that, occasionally, she did entertain fantasies of getting back together with Lance. That he'd take her in his arms and share all the emotions he'd been bottling up and confess that he'd never stopped loving her. Because that was the secret pain Erin carried. She might have divorced him but she hadn't stopped loving him.

Lance should have known it wouldn't take Erin long to rip into him for deciding to work. But she didn't understand what was at stake here. And while a small voice in the back of his head told him she would understand if he would just tell her, he reminded that voice that he didn't owe her anything anymore.

When she set the plate of Della's pastries and the giant mug of hot cocoa in front of him, he kind of felt bad, seeing the look on her face. He'd hurt her. And sometimes, when his counselor made him look at the reasons why his marriage might have fallen apart, he would privately admit that he knew that expression. He'd wounded her and, for all the dozens of times he said he was sorry, he knew she wanted more from him. He just couldn't give it.

As he munched on a cookie, trying to decipher the financial details swimming before him in one of the spreadsheets, he could hear his dad's voice in the back of his head telling him that only losers cried over girls.

He'd been seven. The little girl who'd lived next door, who'd been his best friend, had moved away. Lance had cried, which was when his dad had given him that first loser speech.

Over the years his dad had told him about other things that defined losers. And Lance was desperately trying not to be one.

Loser Lance. He could still hear his dad's taunts. What would he say now, knowing that Loser Lance was struggling to keep his place in his business? After Lance's divorce, he had overheard his dad make a snide comment to his brother, Ed Junior, at a family dinner about losers not being able to keep their wives. Lance had known whom he was talking about. Him.

He tried to be like Junior, living in the perfect house, with the perfect wife, the perfect family and owning his own company. Of course, Ed Junior's company wasn't really Ed Junior's, but their father's. Their father had built up the business and then Junior had just stepped in. Lance had built his from the ground up, a feat that had earned him grudging recognition from his father. To be forced out now would make him a loser again.

He swallowed the pain that inevitably came with thinking of his family. He'd never shared any of this with Erin, at least not the loser part. She'd had to go to all the disgusting family events where his father paraded Junior around like he was a hero and picked on Lance. His father had tried playing the comparison game with Erin, but when he'd commented about her not being as thin as Junior's wife, Erin had told him it was a good thing she wasn't married to Junior then. Lance had always admired that about her, her confidence in herself and how she'd never let his father's antics rattle her.

In his head, he knew it was ridiculous to play these games with his father, or to let his father's opinion of him matter so much.

But he also knew, at least from his counseling sessions, that his father had shaped a lot of who Lance was. Not just in his drive to succeed. He'd always promised himself to be a better man than his father had been.

He could hear the sound of Erin and the boys laughing in the other room over a mixed-up train delivery. He couldn't remember his father ever playing with him, or even Junior, for that matter. How many hours had Lance spent this past week on his hands and knees helping the boys build their train village and letting the trains go around the track?

He'd played a lot with Lily, too, but not as much.

For once that thought didn't make him as sad as it used to. He could look back on those moments and treasure each one of them, just as he would the ones he'd been sharing with the boys. If he could go back and do anything differently, he would have played with Lily more.

As he tried focusing on the numbers on the screen, the disappointment on Erin's face when he'd told Ryan he couldn't play stared back at him.

She didn't understand.

What was he supposed to do? Save his place in his business, the only chance he had at succeeding in life, or make a few more memories with these little boys?

What did it matter, anyway? He'd be gone in a week and who knew when he would be able to see them again.

His resolve strengthened by the answer of the unknown, the spreadsheets started to make sense. He could see the accounts and how small amounts were being drained, written off as rounding errors. But a dollar here and a dollar there added up quickly.

The only thing he didn't see in the documents Chad had sent was where the money was going. Yes, Janelle had authorized every single one of those transactions, yet it wasn't clear what had happened after. Shouldn't they have also been able to find that money?

Lance pulled up his browser and did a search for Janelle. According to property records, she owned a small condo in one of Denver's less expensive neighborhoods. If she'd been stealing money from them, why didn't she live in a nicer neighborhood?

Her pictures on social media all indicated a modest lifestyle. Though she hadn't updated anything over the past few days, probably out of shame of having lost her job, Lance found it hard to believe that she would have stolen all that money and not used it.

As he looked at the numbers once more, it was easy to understand why Chad would have thought she'd stolen the money. He could even see why it would have been an easy assumption and why Chad wouldn't necessarily have had time to look more deeply at the truth. Chad always liked results, whereas Lance was content with playing more of a long game. It's why they'd made such a good team.

When he finally stretched and closed his laptop, Erin came into the kitchen to make dinner.

"You don't have to quit on my account," she said. "The boys were begging me to play campout, like we did last winter when the power went out, so we're going to roast hot dogs and marshmallows in the fireplace."

She hesitated slightly then added, "You're welcome to join us if you like, but don't feel obligated. There's plenty of other things you can heat up in the fridge."

He knew she was trying to be accommodating and he realized all the times she'd done the same for him when they'd been married. Actually, it had been more than that. Yes, she'd often nagged him about working too much, but there were also the countless times when he'd been working in his study and she'd come in with a plate for him and a quick squeeze. He'd enjoyed the feeling that he was completely and deeply loved by her.

Until now, he couldn't think of a time when he'd ever taken care of her like that.

When he didn't answer, she walked over to the fridge and pulled out the hot dogs. Then she turned and looked at him. "There's some of that pasta left over from last night, or there's stuff to make sandwiches. Do you want me to fix something for you?"

How had he let her go? She was injured and he was supposed to be taking care of her, but here she was, trying to take care of him.

He could still remember her tears as she'd explained why she'd needed to leave him. She'd needed more than just a roof over her head and all the bills paid. She'd needed someone to care about her and grieve with her, not blame her. Someone to share her life with.

Sharing a life was more than just coexisting in the same space, which was one of the things she'd tried to tell him. But he'd closed himself off, not wanting to share those deeper pieces for fear she'd find him lacking.

He watched as Erin closed the refrigerator, put the hot dogs into a bowl and then bustled around the kitchen, gathering the other items she'd need for her time with the boys.

"Well," she said, "you know where we are if you want to join us."

As she turned to leave, he said, "Wait."

She stopped and looked at him. "Are you okay? I know you sometimes get deeply lost in thought when you're working, but you seem different."

He was different. The time apart, this time together, and being faced with losing everything else in his life was playing tricks with his mind.

"I'd like to join you. Just give me a moment to put my stuff away and I'll be right there."

The softening in her expression made him glad he'd stopped her. She gave him a smile, like she was happy he'd agreed to join them. As she walked into the other room, her step was a little lighter, as it had been back when things were good between them.

He missed that about her. He missed a lot of things about her. Even though he was still upset with her for all the bad things that had come between them, he wondered if maybe there was something he could have done differently that would have changed the outcome. And the tiny voice of the little boy afraid to be called a loser wondered if maybe there was the slightest chance she might give things between them another try.

Chapter Six

The boys had fallen asleep in front of the fire and Erin hated to move them. She also hated the idea of leaving the spot where she and Lance had been sitting all evening. It was like the weirdness in the car, and then later in the kitchen, had never happened. In fact, it was almost like their divorce had never happened. Being with Lance could be so completely comfortable at times.

The soft sound of Christmas carols played in the background and even though Lance had always told her he didn't enjoy them much, she'd noticed him humming along to some of the tunes. "Silent Night" came on and Erin looked over at Lance, who wore a wistful expression on his face. She started singing along and he turned and smiled at her.

"I've always loved the sound of your voice," he said.

"Well maybe we'll cross another item off my list and do some Christmas caroling."

She almost wished she hadn't said anything. The smile left his face and he shrugged. "If by Christmas caroling, you mean walking through a neighborhood and singing songs? No. It's too much for you so soon after your injury and I don't want you to have any setbacks."

The compassion on his face was evident and it was hard not to remember the caring man she'd married.

"I was just thinking we could sit around here and sing songs. But if you wanted to, we could join my Bible study group when they go to the nursing home for carols with the residents tomorrow."

As soon as the words were out of her mouth, she chided herself for making such a ridiculous offer. The last thing Lance would do was join in on a church activity.

He smiled. "Do you often do things at the nursing home?"

"About once a month. Each group in our church takes a turn so we have someone going there every week. A lot of them are old-timers whose families have moved away or who don't have any to speak of. They don't want to leave the area where they grew up, so we try to be a family to them."

"That sounds like something you'd be involved in," Lance said. "I always loved how you work so hard to make everyone part of your family. That was the hardest thing for me after our divorce. Even though it was just you and your sisters, I always wished I'd had a family like yours. I felt loved, included and accepted. I wish…" He turned away and stared into the fire.

Erin wanted to ask him what he wished, but she recognized that look on his face and knew he wasn't going to tell her.

"Family is what you make it," she said. "When Leah packed us up and moved us out of the Colonel's house, she told us that we didn't need our father or the constant parade of women he said would be our new mothers to make us a family. We would be our own family and we would be a family to anyone who needed it. So create your own family. Yes, as sisters, we kind of already were. But over the years, whenever someone needed a family, we always stepped in to do that for them."

Knowing how much Lance missed her family, could she find a way for them to be family to him? Or would it be too weird, given their past? She didn't even know how her sisters were going to react to having Lance back in her life again. She hadn't had to tell them yet, since they'd both opted for cruises in different parts of the world. It was too expensive to call home and check in all the time, and they'd agreed not to do so unless it was an emergency.

"You used to even invite Chad over for holidays," Lance said. "You hardly knew me that first year in college, when you invited me to Thanksgiving."

They'd been barely acquaintances but they'd spent time together at Thanksgiving. Getting to know one another as a result had been the beginning of their falling in love.

"You had nowhere else to go," she said.

He gave her another smile that melted her heart. "And that is what I have always loved about you."

The warmth radiating from him made it seem almost impossible that they'd ever split up. For the first time in a long time, they were talking about the past without it being ugly. Sitting here with him, it almost felt like the way things were before everything had gone bad between them.

Her leg was falling asleep and she knew she shouldn't stay in this position much longer.

When she started to get up, the movement was awkward and, with her arm in the cast, she couldn't pull herself up the way she wanted to.

"Let me help you," Lance said. As he'd done multiple times over the past week, Lance pulled her up. Only this time, she lost her balance and fell into him. Maybe it was wrong to linger, but she couldn't help thinking that he still smelled the same way and his arms felt so comforting.

"Do you think I was too hasty in divorcing you?"

The question slipped out before she had the chance to take it back. She'd thought it many times over the past week. But she'd never said anything. Didn't want to get his hopes up or to lead him on. Or worse, end up back in a bad situation.

"I don't know," he said, pulling her close to him. "Some days I miss you and wonder how you could have left me. But other days I think about how much you hurt me and I'm glad it's over."

He led her to the couch in the library. "I keep thinking about what you said about what a marriage needs."

He hesitated, as though he was afraid to talk to her. As he always did when the subject of their relationship came up.

She took his hand. "It's okay. Even if you think I won't like what you have to say, I still want to hear it. You always act like you think I'm going to reject you."

At his dejected look, she knew she'd hit the nail on the head. Worse, she realized that in leaving him, that's exactly what she'd done.

"I'm sorry. You were afraid that if you opened up to me, I'd leave you. You opened up to me about how you blamed me for Lily's death. And then I left."

Once again he didn't respond, but his long sigh told her that was exactly how he'd seen it.

"I wouldn't have left if you'd been willing to move beyond the blame," she said. "Blame is a natural part of the grieving process, but you never wanted to work through it with me. Instead of talking about how much you missed her, or how you missed what we had, the only feelings you ever discussed were the ones of being angry with me for letting Lily die."

Maybe she had been wrong in giving up so easily. But there'd been only so much "it's your fault" that she could take without losing her mind.

"I don't know how to open up about my feelings," Lance finally said. "You've always made it sound so easy, but you've always been close to your sisters. Anything I ever had to say was used against me, either by Junior or my father. Only losers had feelings."

She'd heard his brother call him Loser Lance before, and she'd heard his father laugh. But Lance had always rolled his eyes and acted like he was laughing it off, too. She hadn't realized how deeply those words hurt him.

Suddenly a lot of things about Lance made sense.

She gave his hand a squeeze. "Only insecure men who don't know how to deal with their own emotions would call someone a loser for having feelings. That's probably a great discussion to have with your counselor."

Lance smiled weakly. "She had me make a list of all the ways in which I was a winner. But it seems like no matter what I do, I keep hearing my father in the back of my head, telling me what losers did or didn't do."

Even though he'd made his feelings about his faith

clear, she couldn't help telling him, "God doesn't think you're a loser. And He would never call you one. Maybe you have the wrong picture of what a father is supposed to look like in your head."

"Only losers believe in an invisible God," Lance muttered. "And when Lily died, I wondered if maybe I was being punished for being a loser."

Erin couldn't help herself. She put her arms around him and gave him a warm hug. "You were not being punished. And you aren't a loser," she said, holding him close to her.

He rested his head on her shoulder and closed his eyes. "I wish I could believe that."

She couldn't think of anything to say that would help him see that he wasn't a loser. But at least now she could understand his pain and anger.

Lord, please give Lance what he needs. And if there's something I can do, please show me.

She kissed the top of his head and gave him a squeeze. "I'm sorry I never realized how much their nickname hurt you. I was your wife, and I was blind to it. I know it's no excuse, but I think it's because I've never seen you as a loser. You were always the handsomest, smartest, kindest man I've ever known."

Lance opened his eyes and looked at her. "You saw me as a winner?"

"I don't see people as winners or losers. We're all at different stages in life, and it's not fair to treat it like a competition. But I always thought you were very successful."

His nod made her realize that his drive for success, his immersion into his company, was always part of his desire to shed his loser status. She'd seen it as a job, but he'd seen it as his identity.

He gave her a weird smile. "You know why I'm here?'

"To make peace with our past?"

Lance shrugged. "That's what my counselor said I had to do. But do you know why I went to a counselor?"

"Because you finally realized you needed help?"

"Nope." Lance pulled away and straightened. "Because Chad said that my emotional state was interfering with my ability to run the company, and that if I didn't get help and wasn't cleared by a counselor to return to work, he was going to force me out."

Erin closed her eyes and took a deep breath. Was that her heart beating or his? Did it matter? She'd known he was up to something when he'd first arrived, but her injury, and then his helping her, had mostly pushed those thoughts to the back burner.

But now?

She said a quick prayer for understanding then opened her eyes. "So you helping me was just your way of earning brownie points to make the counselor think we'd made peace so you could get your job back? That's why you were working today? You finally got the okay to start work again."

Her stomach felt tied up in knots. Like someone had punched her over and over. Even though she'd thought she'd put a respectable amount of distance between them, the blows kept coming.

This was all her fault. She was the one who'd opened up to him, asked him about their marriage and asked him to share with her.

"Mostly," he said. "I don't know."

He looked like he was about to cry, but in all the years she'd known Lance, Erin had never seen him do so.

"I helped you because it was the right thing to do. And, yes, I have wondered if this is what making peace with you looked like. I've checked in with my counselor a couple of times, and she seemed happy that I was helping you and we were getting along."

Erin had seen him go off to make a phone call or two during his stay, but hadn't asked him about it since she'd figured he was entitled to his privacy.

Even though Lance had never been the kind of man to lie, she knew he was adept at hiding what he really thought or felt. She supposed he'd needed to be if his family continually referred to him as a loser.

But she'd never demeaned him in any way. So why couldn't he have just told her the truth?

"As far as the business goes, I checked my email while I was at the café. I found out some things that bothered me, so I called Chad. We talked and he's letting me come back in a small way. Which is what I was working on tonight."

She believed his explanation about work, since it was the only thing that made sense in terms of his time off and his sudden need to work on a project today. But in his sharing of the facts, he seemed to default to not being open with her about how he was feeling.

"Why tell me now?"

Lance shrugged. Erin pulled away to twist sideways to face him.

"No, you don't get to do that. If you're really here to make peace with me, then you need to face all those big, scary emotions you're so desperate to avoid. The only reason I have ever been your adversary is that you've closed yourself off to me. Maybe it's time for you to open up and see what it's like to have someone else on your team."

For a moment he looked like he might have wanted to agree with her, but then she saw the same scared-little-boy look on his face that always appeared whenever they were talking about something real. He was afraid she would reject him, but in all of his actions, he'd set himself up for the very thing he feared.

So did she press him on the issue to see if they could finally make headway? What if she did open him up to greater intimacy, to where they finally connected on an emotional level, and he still decided his unforgiveness toward her was too much for him to move beyond?

But that was the very thing she was asking him to do. If she wanted him to take a risk to move past his fears in their relationship, shouldn't she be willing to do the same?

"I know you're scared," she said. "I'm scared, too. What if you can never stop hating me over what happened to Lily? But, if you're willing to try, then so am I. It takes two people to make a marriage work, and I felt like I was the only person willing to invest in our relationship. Maybe I was wrong for saying something now. It seemed like, with everything we've been through, and the changes I've seen in you, that maybe you were more open to the idea."

She'd been watching his face the entire time she'd been speaking, hoping to find some sign that he was receptive. So far he just wore the same sullen expression she remembered from their time in counseling.

Obviously any sign in him that she thought she'd

seen to indicate his willingness to give their relationship another shot was hers and hers alone. She'd been caught up in the fancy of spending time with Lance and the boys and thinking about what their life could have been.

But they couldn't go back. Though she'd tried moving forward, it was clear that the ever-widening gulf between them would keep them from moving forward together.

"I'm sorry," she said, getting up. "I shouldn't have pressed the issue. You're here to help me, and you didn't ask for all this emotional stuff. I'm sorry if I've made you uncomfortable."

For a minute she thought Lance looked like he wanted to say something. But the moment passed, so Erin went to her room. Maybe someday she'd find a way to get over Lance.

Why had he just let her walk away?

He'd also been thinking about how much he was enjoying his time with her and wondering if there was a chance they could try again. He'd been so stupid in his answers to her. When she'd asked him to participate in the discussion, he hadn't been able to say a word.

What was he supposed to say? That, yes, he did want to give things another try, but what if he couldn't be the man she wanted?

True, she had been encouraging when it came to his admission about being Loser Lance. He hadn't known why he'd told her that, because he'd never told her things like that. Even though he'd been met with acceptance, would those feelings remain once they had a disagreement?

And then there was Lily.

It wasn't just that he blamed Erin for Lily's death, because that was starting to get a little more complicated. Part of him said that she was responsible because it was what he had been telling himself all this time. But he also saw how caring and compassionate she was with the boys. How well she watched them. And how, even when she was supposed to be resting or doing other things, she always seemed to have one eye or one ear on them. Maybe it was because she'd learned from their experience with Lily. Or maybe he needed to rethink what it meant to be at fault.

That was the other thing troubling him. The longer he was there with Erin and the boys, the less he thought about his grief. What kind of father was he, so easily forgetting his daughter? It was clear Erin wasn't doing much to keep Lily's memory alive.

He thought her a bad person for that. But was he any better, considering Lily no longer constantly occupied his thoughts the way she used to?

They hadn't turned off the Christmas carols and he could hear "O Holy Night" come on in the other room. It had been Erin's favorite song and he wondered if she could hear in her bedroom.

He went to her room, knocked softly on the door and it opened on its own. Erin was sitting on the bed, her back to him. She was hunched over, clutching something to her chest.

Was she having a heart attack?

He pushed open the door and ran in. "Erin? Are you okay?"

As he raced in, she turned and he saw the tears streaming down her cheeks. She had what looked like a picture frame in her arms. She hadn't been having a heart attack, but she looked like she had been crying as if her heart was breaking. Had it meant that much to her to try to work things out?

"I'm sorry for disturbing you," he said. "I knocked and when you didn't answer, I was worried, so I thought I would check on you. 'O Holy Night' is on, and I know how you love that song."

Tears continued rolling down her cheeks but she didn't say a word. The picture fell from her hands and landed on the bed, giving him a glimpse of the image that had her so upset.

It was the last picture they had taken together as a family—the day before Lily died. As he stared at it, he remembered.

He'd told Erin that he was canceling their plans to go away for the weekend because they were pitching a new supplier. She'd begged him to reconsider because she'd said she had a surprise for him. He'd been grouchy with her and told her he didn't want her stupid surprise. They'd been arguing a lot, and Erin had been asking him to do more with Lily so she could rest, and that had irritated him because she was a stay-at-home mom. Why did she need all this rest, when he was the one out working and providing for them?

At first he couldn't remember why they'd even taken the picture, but then he caught sight of the little snowman in Lily's arms and remembered. Erin had wanted them to do a family picture for their Christmas cards. Even though Christmas had been months away, she'd wanted to do one early for some crazy idea she had. Lance had been too irritated with her to find out. Funny how the little things like that came back to him.

She wanted to give their relationship another try, but that was based on now, when they were getting along, not like times in the past when they'd both been irritated with each other. In the picture, even Lily hadn't been in the best of moods. She'd been cranky and fussy all day. Looking back, he'd been short with Erin over it.

She picked up the picture and held it out to him. "Would you like a better look?"

He shook his head. "I didn't realize you kept any of your pictures. There aren't any on the walls."

She pointed to an open trunk on the other side of the room. "I keep all of her things in there. You're welcome to look through them if you like."

He hadn't thought about where Erin kept Lily's things. Her house now seemed so devoid of any memory of her.

Not that his house was much different. It wasn't like he'd turned it into a shrine to Lily. He'd been so tormented with his memories of her that he hadn't needed to.

"Maybe some other time," he said.

She grabbed a tissue from the nightstand, wiped her eyes and then blew her nose. "Sure. If you want copies of any of the pictures, I'm sure we can work something out."

She'd gotten all of Lily's things in the divorce. At the time he hadn't wanted the reminders. But now he did admit to being a little curious. What had she saved?

She gave him a weary look. "I should probably check on the boys and get them into their own beds."

She pushed herself off the bed like it was a great effort. "Don't," he said. "I'll take care of it. I'll make sure they get to bed and are safely tucked in. You've obviously pushed yourself too hard and need your rest."

It was an easy enough excuse. But as he looked at the lines in her forehead, he knew her fatigue wasn't from exertion but from showing her heart to him and him doing nothing.

He'd done to her exactly what he'd feared she'd do to him.

Their earlier discussion and now seeing her break down would make this the perfect time for Lance to say all the things he'd been afraid to say to her earlier. Instead, he walked out with the excuse of needing to take care of the boys. It wasn't like he'd never seen her cry before. But it always made him uncomfortable. Seeing the depth of her pain made it more real to him. More important, it made him realize that what she had been saying a while back about them comforting each other was true.

But how did you get back to that place? Or even find it, when you hadn't had it to begin with? He didn't know. He wasn't sure there was a way, not after they'd spent so much time hurting one another.

He shook Dylan awake and the sleepy-eyed boy immediately went to his room. Then Lance picked up Ryan, who cuddled against him in such a loving, trusting way that Lance couldn't understand why he couldn't have this for himself.

He didn't think men were supposed to have such deep longings for a child. He knew if he ever expressed anything like this to his father, his father would probably laugh and make fun of him. But as he tucked in the little boy, Lance remembered Erin's words about winners and losers. Could he be basing his identity on something that was meaningless?

His father was a respected businessman. Yet the more Lance thought about it, the more he realized that while people respected his father as a businessman, he didn't actually have friends. He'd never seen his father in the same kind of warm community environment that always seemed to surround Erin and her sisters. Even though Lance had been late picking her up from church, it hadn't bothered her, because she been too busy talking with all her friends.

He also thought about what Erin had said about God not thinking him a loser. How did she know what God thought?

He'd tried faith out for a while, going to church with Erin from time to time, but he hadn't been sure he believed all that stuff, and work provided an easy excuse to get out of going. Now he wished he'd paid a little more attention.

He spied Ryan's Lily bear on the floor. Funny, it didn't hurt anymore, seeing that silly bear. He picked it up and held it in his hands. It was much more worn than it had been with Lily, but he could tell how much the little boy loved it. He'd been unfair in resenting the fact that Lily bear had been given to the little boy who'd just needed some comfort. Clearly, Lily bear had given him just that. In a way, it gave Lance comfort, as well. He tucked the bear in with Ryan and gave Ryan a kiss on top of his head.

He loved the little boy.

Even though he'd been thinking a lot about it, he'd been avoiding the conversation with Erin about what would happen when her sisters returned and he left.

He'd like to see the boys again and have a relationship with them. He'd been afraid to ask because he didn't want to face rejection. Just like he hadn't wanted Erin to reject him again in starting a new relationship. But maybe, over the next few days, he'd find the courage to let Erin know that he would appreciate the opportunity to stay in touch with the boys. Surely that was less threatening than just coming out and telling her how much it meant to him.

It was so crazy, how worried he was about rejection. He'd been running a major company and faced rejection every day as he and Chad had grown their business. But for whatever reason, facing this personal rejection was just too much to ask.

Chapter Seven

The fresh snowfall overnight meant that there would be plenty for the sleigh ride at Ricky's. The beauty of the glistening snow made Erin smile. As Lance drove to the neighboring ranch, he was silent, but the boys were full of excitement, chattering about all the fun things they were going to do at Mr. Ricky's. At least they were oblivious to the tension between Erin and Lance. This was why Erin shouldn't have said anything to him. Why had she gotten caught in that moment of fancy and thinking about how good things used to be between her and Lance? And to have let him see her fall apart like that? He was just supposed to be helping her, and yet, things were getting more complicated than she would have liked.

When they got to Ricky's, the number of cars collected in his driveway indicated a large crowd had already arrived. A lot of businesses in town closed a little early for the day so people could come. Ricky had started the tradition as a way to thank his ranch hands, but every year, the gathering grew. He'd probably invited half the town, or at least the entire church.

He kept telling Erin that he wanted to slow down, do less. Erin now wondered if Ricky actually understood the meaning of the word.

Ricky greeted them warmly when they got into the house. Erin turned and gestured to Lance. "Ricky, I'd like you to meet someone. This is Lance, my ex-husband."

Ricky looked Lance up and down and said, "What kind of fool are you, giving up a good woman like Erin? If I'd found myself a woman like her, you'd better believe I'd never let her go."

She should have known that Ricky would have said something inappropriate. But when she looked at Lance to see his reaction, it didn't appear to have bothered him. A good sign, because she hadn't brought Lance here to be made to feel bad about their divorce. At least now Lance had met Ricky and understood he wasn't a threat.

Not that Lance had any reason to feel threatened. She'd made it clear that she was interested in rekindling the relationship, but he pushed her away. So even though Lance occasionally acted like he was jealous, he also didn't have the right to be.

Erin had spent too many years fighting to make the marriage work when she seemed to be the only person in that marriage who'd made it a priority. If she'd learned anything from watching her sisters in their new relationships, it was that there were men willing to treat a marriage as give-and-take, and they were equally invested in making the relationship work.

Lance hadn't given her any indication of what he wanted. Maybe he didn't know. And then there was the business situation. What was she supposed to make of that? It had meant a lot to her, having him around. But now she couldn't help wondering if his kindness toward her was genuine or just part of a ploy to score points with his counselor to get back in Chad's good graces.

Ricky led them into the great room, where many of Erin's friends and neighbors had gathered. It was going to be weird, explaining Lance to all of them, but the women in her Bible study group yesterday at church had been understanding when she'd done so there.

The boys ran off to play with the other children. Wanda, Ricky's housekeeper, had set up a station for the children to decorate their own gingerbread cookies.

As Erin went to join her friends, she noticed Lance hung back.

"Join us," she said. "My friends are great people, and you'll enjoy getting to know them."

"Maybe I should just pick you up later," he said. "It doesn't look like you need my help here."

He looked like the scared little boy from last night, confessing his insecurities but not brave enough to face them.

"You can leave if you want," she said. "But then you'll miss out on all the fun. I'd like you to stay. But that's up to you. I don't want to make you uncomfortable. At least let me introduce you."

Oddly enough, she realized she did want him to stay. She hadn't been lying when she'd said she thought he'd enjoy the activities. Maybe it was wrong of her to want to spend more time with Lance, having fun, especially since she knew this couldn't last. But maybe, even though he wouldn't be with her, Lance would learn to live again.

"Travis Marshall, my friend Angela's husband, is

into rock climbing. You two could trade stories," she said. She emphasized the part about Travis being her friend's husband. Hopefully by pointing out people Lance would enjoy spending time with, it would make him feel more comfortable and more willing to join in.

Lance gave a shrug as he joined her.

When they got to her group of friends, everyone greeted her warmly.

"This is Lance, my ex-husband. I was telling you about him in Bible study. He's been a great help to me and the boys. I'm trying to convince him to stay and join us."

As Erin had predicted, they all started talking at once about how Lance was welcome and how he should stay. Instead of making him more comfortable, he only looked nervous.

Finally, Janie Roberts, one of the ladies who was becoming a good friend of the family, silenced the group and turned to Lance. "I'm sure you must feel awkward, being Erin's ex-husband. If it makes you feel any better, she's never said anything bad about you. If you're here for her, helping her, you've got to be a pretty great guy."

Even though Janie's words were meant to be encouraging, it stung a little for Erin to hear them. Especially since she'd just told Lance that she'd thought about giving them another try. But at least Lance would understand that he wasn't walking into a group of people who hated him.

If only she could read his expression to tell how he was taking it.

Lance nodded but he didn't seem any less uncomfortable. He shoved his hands in his pockets and stood at the edge of the group, looking like he still wanted to bolt at any time.

Ryan came running up to him, frosting smeared all over his face, carrying a cookie. “Uncle Lance. Look what I made you.”

He held the cookie out to Lance and Lance knelt to the boy’s height. “Thank you,” Lance said. “He looks too good to eat.”

Dylan joined them. “But you should. They’re delicious. Besides, cookies are meant to be eaten.”

With that, Dylan bit off his cookie’s head and grinned.

Erin couldn’t help laughing. If anyone could bring Lance out of his shell, it was the boys. Once again, it made her sad to think that he had no dreams or plans for the future of becoming a father again. He’d been a great one, except for when he’d been so busy with work.

How could she get Lance to understand how important it was to balance work and family? When he was with the family, focusing on them, he was amazing. But when work intruded, he was a different person.

“Try it,” Ryan said.

Lance took a bite of the cookie and smiled at the boys. “You’re right. It’s delicious. Thank you for sharing your cookie with me.” Lance stood then looked over at the tables where refreshments had been laid out.

“It looks like they have some hot cocoa and cider over there. You want to go with me and get something to drink?” He turned to Erin. “Can I get you anything?”

“That would be great, thanks. Wanda makes the best cider.”

She watched as he took the boys’ hands and went

over to the refreshment table. When Erin or her sisters tried to take the boys' hands, they would inform her that they were too old for such little-boy things. But for whatever reason, maybe it was because they were so attached to Lance, they always eagerly grabbed his hands without him asking. Erin wondered if he knew how much that meant.

Maybe, instead of making the conversation about their relationship, Erin needed to focus more on what was best for the boys. They clearly needed a relationship with their uncle. While Erin was already planning to talk to Leah about facilitating that, she knew it would be easier for everyone if she wasn't making Lance uncomfortable by forcing him to deal with emotions he found difficult.

Janie came up beside her. "You didn't mention how good-looking he was. Or how sweet. Remind me again why you got divorced."

Definitely not the conversation she wanted to have right now, especially since she was trying hard to do the right thing in this situation.

"Because he was emotionally unavailable at a time when I needed him most." She gestured over to the drink table, where Ricky was showing Lance and the boys his rope tricks.

"He's great about physically being here, at least when he's not consumed with work. Maybe I'm asking too much. But I see how happy my sisters are, and I know that it's possible to have a man who is emotionally present."

A thoughtful look crossed Janie's face. "They are hard to come by. My dad has always been so great that it never occurred to me that other men were not as in touch with their feelings. Unfortunately, I learned that the hard way."

She glanced over at her son, who had joined the boys and Ricky. In all the time Erin had known Janie, the single mom had never spoken of her son's father. But watching the expression on her face, Erin figured that's who her friend must have been talking about.

Janie turned back to Erin. "But I got a great kid out of the deal, so I have no regrets. And even though I probably shouldn't have said anything, and you can tell me to butt out if I'm overstepping, I don't know a lot of men who would drop everything to help their ex-wife the way Lance has been helping you. It's obvious you still love him, so maybe you guys can figure out how to make that emotional thing work between you. I don't think he's a lost cause."

Erin had thought the same thing, at least until Lance had shut her down last night.

"Thanks. To be honest, I've been rethinking a lot of things about our relationship. I don't know if anything will come of it, and my main focus is on the boys. But maybe, once my sisters return, Lance and I can figure some of this out."

"I'll be praying for you," Janie said.

Janie gave her a quick hug and they rejoined the group. Everyone was discussing plans to go to the nursing home tomorrow. She'd briefly discussed it with Lance and he hadn't given her a firm answer. But, she supposed, if he didn't want to take her, she and the boys could find a ride.

Lance and Ricky joined them. Ricky wore such a mischievous grin that Erin was almost afraid of what the older man had up his sleeve.

"Erin, you never told us that your ex was *the* Lance Drummond," Ricky said.

She'd never heard of Lance being referred to in such exalted terms.

"I'm not sure what you wanted me to have said about him," she said.

"Well, for starters, he's an expert mountaineer," Ricky noted. "Now you know I've been looking for someone to lead some of the crazies coming to my ranch on mountain climbing expeditions. I could've hired him."

If Lance was interested in a job. Erin smiled at Ricky. "Did he also mention that he owns a very successful outdoor company and it takes up so much of his time that he has little time for climbing?"

"Ultimate Outdoors. I know." Ricky nodded enthusiastically. "I've been trying to get their sales rep to call me back about special pricing for the ranch. If I had known that you knew the owner, I'd have gone straight to the top. We've got a party going on right now, but I expect you to bring Lance back to see me before he leaves town."

She glanced over at Lance, who shrugged like it was no big deal. Maybe this was the good that could come out of the situation. Ricky was known to be a shrewd businessman. One didn't carry on a ranching legacy that had lasted for four generations without that skill. And yet Ricky seemed to know all about balancing his personal life and his professional life—no small feat, considering he lived and breathed the Double R.

Travis, the man Erin had thought Lance would get along well with, stepped forward. "You're Lance Drummond? I love your blog articles on Ultimate Outdoors. That one on first aid in the wilderness? It saved my buddy's life."

It was amazing how quickly people surrounded Lance, talking to him about his business. A lot of the people in the area loved the outdoors. From camping to hiking to rock climbing to fishing to hunting, all were activities popular in the area. So to find that this was not only Lance's passion but his business gave everyone something to talk about.

Watching Lance talk, and seeing the animation on his face as everyone told him about all of the activities to do around Columbine Springs, wasn't helping Erin in her quest to get over him. Their shared love of the outdoors had always given them fun ways to spend time together. That was the thing Erin had missed the most when it came to Lance being so busy with his business. They'd stopped doing a lot of those things.

One of her favorite baby shower gifts when she'd been pregnant with Lily had been a backpack carrier so they could take Lily with them on hikes. But the carrier had remained in the box because Lance was always working too much. Erin hadn't been able to handle getting outdoors with Ryan and Lily plus Dylan all by herself. Leah had been busy working to make ends meet for her family, and Nicole had been working while trying to finish up her masters.

None of this had mattered to Lance, at least not as far as she could tell. Though she'd wondered if he'd ever been lost in the same kind of moments of melancholy where he thought about all the things they could have done but had never gotten around to. She'd brought it up to him once after Lily died, but he'd only gotten angry with her and told her it wasn't his fault they hadn't had the chance to do any of those things with Lily.

What would he say now? Had he done any of the things he used to love during his time off work?

One of the ranch hands came in to let them know the sleigh was ready. Erin gathered the boys and they followed him outside to prepare for their outing.

Lance hadn't expected to enjoy himself so much. His original plan had been to stay long enough to be polite, make excuses to leave, then go back to the house and continue looking through the books. Chad had made good on his promise to send updated passwords, and as far as Lance could tell, everything was good between them. But as they loaded into the horse-drawn sleigh, Lance was glad he'd stayed.

Because so many people had come, not everyone would be able to ride in the sleigh. People seemed to have prepared for that, many had brought snowshoes. Lance had taken Erin snowshoeing once. It had been a lot of fun and he'd always hoped they could do it again. Looking at Erin's foot, it would be a while before she'd be able to do so.

Ricky gestured to a spot in the sleigh. "Erin, you sit there. Lance you get next to her and the boys can sit on your laps."

The arrangement brought them practically snuggled up together. As he caught the gleam in Ricky's eye, Lance was pretty sure Ricky had done that on purpose. As more people piled into the sleigh, Lance was forced to sit even closer to Erin. As a mature adult, it seemed easy enough to handle. After all, he and Erin had been in close proximity often since his arrival.

But then she shivered and Lance couldn't help putting his arm around her. Ricky tossed them a blanket. "I've got a whole stack of them, so you take what you need. We've already got poor Erin on injured reserve, and I don't want her getting sick on top of it." Lance wrapped the blanket around all of them, which made Erin snuggle even closer to him.

Why did she still have to feel so good in his arms? This wasn't the first time he'd been aware of her, remembering things like how he used to tease her that her shampoo smelled like sunshine. It still did.

She whispered something in Ryan's ear, but Lance couldn't hear it because of the wind rushing around them. The fresh snow made for a nice ride, but it was colder out than he'd expected and it made him realize just how long it had been since he'd spent much time outdoors in the winter.

Before he'd gotten so busy with work, he'd done all sorts of adventurous winter outdoor things. It was weird, listening to all these people go on and on about how much they admired him when he wasn't much of a mountaineer or an outdoorsman anymore. Erin used to accuse him of having lost his way. Oddly enough, being here, part of her new life, talking with her new friends, he could kind of understand why.

It seemed crazy to think about how much everything had changed for him in recent years.

Yes, he'd put all the blame on Erin after Lily's death, saying that his life had been just fine, perfect actually, until Erin'd had to go and ruin it all by letting their daughter die. As much as Lance hated to admit it, he'd lost a lot of the things he'd loved long before he'd lost Lily.

Dylan looked up at him. "Uncle Lance?"

"What's up?"

"How come after your daughter died, you and Aunt Erin got a divorce instead of having more kids? You'd make a good dad."

If it hadn't been a nine-year-old kid asking him that question, Lance would've punched him. Especially because Erin's indrawn breath told him the innocent question hadn't just been a punch to his gut but had hurt Erin, as well.

Instead, Lance gave him a squeeze, trying to find the right words without breaking down.

"It's not that simple," he finally said. But Dylan continued staring at him like he expected an answer.

Out of the corner of his eye, Lance glanced at Erin, who was clearly trying not to cry. The question was probably doubly painful for her, considering she'd just asked Lance to consider giving their relationship another try.

Lance took a deep breath. "Have you ever tried your hardest at something, only it still didn't work?"

Dylan nodded. "I really wanted to be the pitcher, but coach keeps putting me in outfield."

Not exactly the same thing. "Do you keep trying to be the pitcher or do you just do the best job you can as an outfielder?"

Dylan gave him a stubborn look. "My dad says you never give up on your dreams."

A great motivational speech if you weren't talking about losing your family.

"Your dad sounds like a wise man. But sometimes you have to evaluate whether or not your dream is really possible. And when it comes to people, and relationships, it's a lot harder than just going out in the backyard and throwing more balls."

Dylan rested his head on Lance's chest. "Well, I think you should think about having more kids. You'd be a really good dad and Aunt Erin would be the best mom, besides my mom."

A tear ran down Erin's cheek and Lance watched as she quickly brushed it away.

He'd been so foolish in thinking that Lily's death had been all about him and his loss.

Lance gave Dylan another squeeze. "Thank you. That's high praise, coming from a wise kid. I'll tell you what. Why don't you leave these grown-up matters to the grown-ups, and you focus on becoming the best baseball player you can?"

Dylan snorted. "I'm not going to be a baseball player. I'm going to be a cowboy. The baseball part is just for fun. When I grow up, I'm going to have a bigger ranch than Mom and Dad's, and even Mr. Ricky's. Everyone is going to say I have the nicest cows in the whole wide world, and my horses are going to be the prettiest and smartest."

Ricky turned from his spot in the driver's seat. "Bigger than mine? That's some ambition you got, boy."

Ricky chuckled and Lance was grateful for the way it lightened the moment, because even Erin had smiled.

When he'd come, he'd been angry with her for suggesting that she might find love again and start a new family. But the longing on her face after Dylan's comment was real. He'd made Lily's loss all about him, but after last night, and now, he could see how wrong he'd been.

Erin had suggested they try again on their relationship.

But it hadn't worked before and he hadn't been able to be the man she'd wanted. So what made her think he could be now?

Chapter Eight

Lance hung back as a group went to cut Christmas trees. He looked around for Erin and the boys but didn't see them. Ricky stepped up beside him. "They're fine. Erin's in the warming hut over by the pond, and the boys went with the others to get trees. Jack, my foreman, is watching out over them. Erin looked like she could use a break and, after the conversation in the sleigh, I figured you could use one, too." Ricky held up a thermos. "Want some coffee?"

Lance nodded and Ricky unscrewed the cap and handed it to him. He poured some coffee into that cup then pulled a folding cup out of his jacket pocket.

"We sell a lot of those in our stores," Lance said. "Very handy."

Ricky grinned. "That's where I got it. Always loved your stuff. You might not be the cheapest outfit around, but you get what you pay for."

He liked Ricky's no-nonsense way of putting things.

"That's always been the point of Ultimate Outdoors," Lance said. "My friend Chad and I started the company after we'd gone on a camping trip and the equipment we bought at one of those big box stores failed. We talked to the company, but they didn't care. So, we started our own business, finding the best equipment out there. People liked it, and the business grew faster than either of us could have imagined."

He felt like an idiot, rambling on about the business, except Ricky seemed interested. Whenever he'd talked about work, Erin had always seemed to zone out. Even being here, with Lance finally having an opportunity to prove himself, Erin had gotten defensive when he'd tried to tell her about it.

One more reason he wondered how they would make it work a second time if it had been such a problem for her during their marriage. He still needed to make a living. And now that he'd spent part of the day with her and her friends, he couldn't see her being willing to give this up to move back to Denver with him.

"It's like a good woman," Ricky said. "Once you find one, you don't want to let her go."

He should have known he was walking right into something. It was plain to see that the old man cared deeply for Erin and her family. Lance was glad that the sisters had finally found a father figure they could count on.

Lance smiled at Ricky. "A good woman is a treasure indeed, but just because she's a good woman doesn't mean she's the right woman for every man."

Ricky didn't return his smile. "How'd you let her go?"

"She left me," Lance said.

"What'd you do to make her leave? Erin isn't the type to walk away from a commitment. She's the most loyal woman I know."

His father had asked him that same question, for the same reasons. Except his father had also made snide comments about how he figured Lance couldn't keep a woman like Erin. But Lance could tell by the look on Ricky's face that he wasn't so much judging him as trying to understand.

Lance drank the rest of his coffee. "She said I wasn't emotionally available."

"My Rosie used to complain about the same thing. And my boy, Cinco. They both said I cared more about the ranch than I did about them. And it took losing them for me to realize they were right."

The older man's weathered face was filled with regret. "Don't make the same mistake I did. I know you two lost a child, but you're young. I know another child can never replace what you lost, but I'll tell you I'd give just about anything for the chance to be a father, or even a grandfather. My son's wife was pregnant when he died, but because we didn't have a good relationship, I didn't even get to meet my grandchild. Erin and her sisters are helping me try to locate him or her, but we keep running into dead ends."

Listening to Ricky, Lance understood what the other man was trying to do. To help him see the mistakes he'd made so he could rectify them before he got to be Ricky's age and it was too late.

"But that doesn't mean Erin and I can make it work," Lance said.

Ricky nodded slowly. "Do you love her?"

Lance sighed. It wasn't that simple. And, mostly, he wasn't sure. Sometimes he thought he still loved her. But other times he was so angry with her, he thought he might hate her.

"You do," Ricky said. "Love is a complicated emotion. Everyone watching the two of you together can tell you love each other. You've just forgotten how to go about it. Whatever makes you afraid of your emotion, fix it. If you can't figure it out with a good woman like Erin, there's probably not anyone else in this world who can do it for you."

That was exactly why Lance hadn't started dating. Why he couldn't understand why Erin had been so willing to start again. But she wasn't the one who had problems with emotion. She'd do just fine.

"Don't say you're fine being alone. I told that lie for years. Then you watch everyone around you die and you realize, what were you on this earth for? I got me a pile of money and nothing to do with it. Erin's helping me with my trust to preserve the ranch for future generations. What are you going to do with that big old company of yours?"

If he still had a place in the company. Lance figured it would go to Chad, but Chad was in the same position. Too married to his work to find anyone special. There'd been a woman once, before he and Chad had met, but all Chad would say was that he'd learned his lesson and it was enough.

He supposed, if Leah would let him have a relationship with the boys, he could leave it to them, but he had to admit that having a relationship with his quasi nephews was different from having his own family.

So far, Ricky had been doing all the talking and Lance had been answering in his head. But the way Ricky looked at him, Lance knew he was going to have to give an answer sooner or later. Except he didn't have any.

"I know you mean well," Lance finally said. "But I can't give you the answers you're looking for. I can't be the man Erin wants me to be, and I'm not sure how we move past everything that happened between us. I appreciate you taking the time to tell me about your past, but there's nothing I can do at this point."

Ricky nodded slowly. "I guess you're not as smart as I thought you were. But you can't blame an old fool for trying. You should go with that group from the church to visit the nursing home so you can see what you have to look forward to. Because that's the life you're choosing."

Lance didn't need the old man's reminder, but as he thought about his words, he figured the nursing home was exactly where he'd end up. Having a family didn't necessarily mean he wouldn't be there anyway. Sometimes he thought about his grandmother, dying in one of those places all alone. He'd been wanting to tell Erin that he would go caroling with them at the nursing home, but he hadn't yet found the nerve. He didn't want to get her hopes up that it meant anything other than keeping a long-ago promise made to himself to not let people in nursing homes be forgotten. And yet, until Erin had asked him about going with them, he hadn't thought of that promise in years. So much for all his good intentions.

Ricky held his hand out to Lance for the top of his thermos. "I'd best be getting on to check on my other guests. Sorry to have wasted your time."

He hated the dejected tone to Ricky's voice, but he couldn't bring himself to make a promise he couldn't keep.

"Thanks for the company. I appreciate you sharing your wisdom, even if I don't think it applies to me right now."

Ricky gave a quick nod and walked off to chat with some of the others mingling in the area. Lance walked over to the warming hut, not specifically to join Erin, but he did want to know how she was doing after the sleigh ride. Just because he did not see a way to be with her didn't mean he didn't still care about her.

Her friend Janie was in the hut with her and it was clear Erin had been crying.

"I'm sorry," he said. "I'll come back. I just wanted to make sure you're okay."

Janie stood and patted the seat she'd been occupying. "No. You stay. I should go. The tree cutting party should be back soon and I want to check on the boys."

Lance looked over at Erin, who nodded. "Please," she said.

He sat and Erin looked at him with such sadness, it made his heart ache. "What Dylan said to you earlier upset me because of something you don't know. Janie convinced me that it wasn't good to hide it or keep it a secret."

A slew of horrible possibilities ran through his mind and his stomach clenched.

"You can tell me anything," he said.

Erin squeezed his hands. Hers were warm and his felt so cold after being outside. He hadn't been wearing gloves, he should have known better.

"Let me get you warmed up," Erin said. She reached beside her for a thermos of coffee, but Lance shook his head. "I'm fine. Ricky shared some of his with me."

"Ricky shared his coffee? You must've really made

an impression on him. He gets his own special thermos of coffee and he doesn't share with anyone."

Though he knew she was trying to impress upon him how much Ricky liked him, it only made Lance feel worse for letting the man down. That seemed to be something he was good at. Letting others down.

"Anyway," Erin continued, "I don't even know how to say this. I never thought I'd tell you."

This was worse than that moment she'd fallen from the ladder and briefly been unconscious.

"You can tell me anything," he repeated.

Erin sighed. "Lily wasn't the only child we lost. I was pregnant when she died. With the stress of everything, I lost the baby. I hadn't told you because you were so angry and then you went out of town on that business trip, and that's when it happened. Nicole took me to the hospital and stayed with me. We got home just before you did."

She'd been pregnant? And she hadn't told him? It felt like all the air had been sucked out of his lungs and he was gasping for breath, except he couldn't even make that effort.

Tears filled her eyes. "There just never seemed to be a good time to tell you. I was going to tell you when we were taking pictures, except you were so angry and impatient, snapping at me for wasting your time, so I thought I'd wait to tell you when you were in a better mood. Then Lily died and you kept saying how irresponsible I was. I just couldn't find a way to say there'd be another baby. But then there wasn't, and I figured you'd blame me for that, too, even though the doctor said there was likely some kind of problem with the baby anyway that caused the miscarriage."

Erin sniffled and said, "That's why I was crying last night, over that picture. I was thinking about Lily and the baby… It was supposed to be our pregnancy announcement."

She was openly sobbing now and Lance just felt numb. He'd had to face so many difficult emotions already. But to learn he'd lost another child? One he hadn't even known about?

"Was it a boy or girl?"

Erin stopped crying and looked at him. "It was too early to tell. The nurse said that sometimes it was easier if you gave the baby a name to mourn it, and I was kind of hoping for a boy, so I called him Noel. It just sort of fit because of when the baby was due."

She'd named their baby Noel. And now the tiny stuffed snowman that she'd insisted on being in the picture made sense. It wasn't a family picture for the Christmas cards. It was an announcement that they were expecting a baby at Christmas, but he'd been too much of a jerk for her to tell him.

Would it have turned out differently if he hadn't been so short tempered with her that weekend? Looking back, he'd been irritated with her because all she'd seemed to want to do was sleep, which was typical for pregnant women. Only he hadn't known she was pregnant and, of course, Erin would want to tell him in some special way. If he'd known she was pregnant, he liked to think he'd have been a little bit nicer to her and taken care of her. Maybe he wouldn't have gone to work that day and maybe Lily wouldn't have…

Lance shook his head. He wasn't going to go there. Couldn't go there. It hurt too much to think about. That was why he didn't understand how Erin had moved on so easily.

"If the baby was due at Christmas, how can you still love Christmas so much?"

She shrugged. "Because Christmas is a time of hope. I don't have my babies, but I can still choose joy, hope and peace. Choosing not to live because they died doesn't honor them in any way. So instead, I make the most of the time I have. While the new memories won't replace the ones I lost, I might as well have something good to go with the bad."

Then she gave him a soft smile. "But that doesn't mean I don't long for things. I want more children. I want a husband to love me. I'm sorry if I made you uncomfortable by asking you to give us another try. I know we can never reclaim what we lost, but I'd like to think that there was good between us, and if we tried, we could make it good again."

"I can't be the man you want me to be," he said, repeating what he'd been telling himself and what he'd told Ricky. This new information didn't change any of it, it just gave him more reason to grieve and more reason to realize how he'd failed her in the past.

She nodded slowly. "Maybe that's true. Like I said, I didn't mean to burden you with any of this. My feelings, the baby and everything else. I still believe we can help each other with our grief, but I know it's too uncomfortable for you. And I'm sorry for pushing you to be someone you don't want to be."

Then she sighed. "I thought that if you loved me, you'd be able to open up to me. But the opposite of that, and also true, is that if I loved you, I would accept you for who you are and not expect you to share your emotions. So maybe this is for the best. Maybe neither of us loves each other the way we think we did."

She stood and leaned down to give him a hug. "Thank you for taking care of me. Whatever the counselor needs from me to say that you're fit to go back to work, it's yours. I think we both have the answers we need. Our marriage wasn't meant to be. And I promise I won't ask you to sell the house again. When you're ready, we can sell it together, or you can buy me out."

When she walked away, it hurt more than watching her leave the courthouse after their divorce. That had been final, but this was even more so. And it felt like it was ripping him in two.

She'd never thought she'd tell Lance about Noel. But she'd been feeling melancholy last night and then today, with what Dylan said, it all just came out. Janie had said that telling Lance was the right thing to do, but seeing the pain on his face, she wasn't so sure.

Erin stepped out of the warming hut just in time to be greeted by a bunch of snowy boys. Their laughter brought a smile to her face, and even though she was hurting, she needed to focus on them. Tonight she'd settle in for a long soak in the claw-foot tub and have another cry.

As much as Lance had come to make peace with her, it was clear she still needed to make peace with their past, as well. She could admit now that she'd been unwilling to date because a small part of her was always hoping that they'd somehow find their way back together. The past two days made her realize that it wasn't going to happen.

So maybe, when Lance left, her heart could break

once and for all and she could find happiness with someone else.

But that thought made her sick.

"Mr. Ricky has all kinds of trees that would make great Christmas trees," Dylan said. "I don't know why we have to wait for Mom and Dad to get back to get our last one. Wouldn't it be great for them to come home and see that we'd gotten one all by ourselves?"

She gave the little boy a squeeze and smiled. "Yes, which is why we're decorating the whole house. But getting a Christmas tree and decorating it together is a family tradition, and we do it as a family."

"Can Uncle Lance come?" Dylan asked.

Erin glanced back at the warming hut. Lance hadn't come out yet.

"We'll see," she said. "I don't know how long he can stay."

Dylan kicked at a pile of snow. "That means no. You always say 'we'll see' when you really mean no."

"It means we'll see. I can't make plans for him." She reached forward and ruffled his hair. "And where is your hat? It's cold out and I don't want you getting sick."

"In my pocket." Dylan pulled it out and showed it to her.

Janie joined them, shaking her head. "I told you to put it on."

Dylan groaned and did as she asked before running off to join the others.

"How'd things go with Lance?" Janie asked.

Erin shrugged. "He didn't say much, as usual. He wanted a few details, and I gave them to him. But I think telling Lance made me realize just how different we are and how much more work it would take to ever get us back together."

"I'm sorry," Janie said. "I was hoping that telling him would bring the two of you closer."

Erin shrugged. "Not if it means opening up emotionally. But thanks for trying."

She turned and looked over at the warming hut. Lance had stepped out and was chatting with Travis. He looked happy, and Erin supposed that was the upside of not being willing to dig into the deeper emotions. He could hear what was devastating to her and then happily go on with his life moments later.

If anything, it was further confirmation that Lance wasn't the man for her. She needed a man who could handle sharing his emotions and working through them together. And he needed a woman who could love him without the complication of all those feelings getting in the way. That made her resolve to find a way to keep Lance in the boys' lives even more difficult. When he met that woman, Erin wasn't sure she could handle it.

Chapter Nine

Lance was surprisingly eager to join them for caroling at the nursing home the next day. They hadn't spoken about anything of import since their time at Ricky's yesterday. But there wasn't anything left to say on the subject. Erin had agreed to give him what he needed, and even though he hadn't said it, that also included his space.

Erin looked up from the craft she was doing with the group of ladies to see Lance talking to an older woman who'd been sitting by herself. They were deep in conversation, and Erin could tell that Lance had made the woman stay. She forced herself to look away, not wanting to give herself any more reason to like him more.

"Look at my reindeer," Edna, the lady she'd been helping, said with pride. Erin often found herself partnered with Edna for activities, and the sweet woman had become very dear to her.

Erin smiled. "You should send that to your daughter in Denver. Maybe she'll put it on her tree."

"She only wants checks from me," Edna said, throwing down the reindeer. "She never calls, except to ask for money. I haven't seen her in nearly two years."

This was why their church's ministry was so important. People like Edna needed to know that someone cared about them.

Erin picked up the reindeer. "I think it's beautiful. So if you don't hang it on your tree, I hope you'll let me put it on mine."

Not that she had room on her personal tree that she kept in the study. It was already overflowing with ornaments, and Lance scowled at it every time he walked by. At least he wouldn't be around to witness the family tree. Even though the boys were really hoping he would stay for them to cut it and decorate it together, she wasn't sure he could handle it.

"I'll put it on my tree," Edna said, snatching it out of her hand. "Now I'm going to go over to the other group and make me a snowman."

The rest of the group at her table had also finished the reindeer, so they all got up to go to some of the other craft stations to make something else. They'd planned to make an afternoon of it, doing various crafts, then later, after supper, singing Christmas carols around the tree. She'd only told Lance about the carols part and, when he'd made it clear he was coming, she'd had to explain that it was going to be an all-day activity.

A day that he spent in the corner with Mary, who never participated in any of their activities. But maybe, having Lance there would make her want to join in.

Erin got up and went over to them. "I have room at the reindeer table if you'd like to make your own reindeer," Erin said.

Mary glared at her. "What would I want with a reindeer? They put me in here to die and it's not like I can take a reindeer with me."

"It's just something pretty to brighten your room. And it's kind of fun, doing crafts." She kept her tone light, trying to be cheerful.

"I don't do crafts," Mary said. "And I hate Christmas."

No wonder Mary and Lance were getting along so well.

"Why do you hate Christmas?" Erin asked.

Mary gestured at the craft tables. "All the commercialism. It's just an excuse for people to make and buy more junk they don't need. When I was a little girl, it was all about family, being together, caring about each other. And where's my family now? Probably up in Aspen, shopping and skiing to their hearts' delight. I'll probably get a package from them, with some junk I'll just regift to one of the nurses because I have no use for it. All those scented lotions and soaps. They give me a rash."

Put that way, Erin could see why Mary hated Christmas. "I can understand that," Erin said. "To be honest, I've never been comfortable with that aspect, either. All the stores, sales, buying a bunch of stuff for people they don't really want or need. That's why our family is intentional about gift giving, and we make it about finding something special for the other person."

At Lance's snort, she continued. "But I will admit that I absolutely love the decorations. It's so beautiful to see all the lights.

"Growing up, we were never allowed decorations. Our father said they were a waste of time and money.

We couldn't even have a Christmas tree. But every year he'd dutifully give us a ridiculous present that seemed to be more about the show of giving us something than it was about doing something nice for us. So my sisters and I promised ourselves that when we could have Christmas without him, we would do whatever made us happy, as long as whatever we did in terms of gifts or something had a special meaning."

As she spoke, Lance's face had softened. "I didn't know that about you. You never told me that story about your father."

Erin shrugged. "I generally don't tell a lot of stories about my father. He wasn't a very nice man."

"I hate Christmas for a lot of the same reasons as Mary," Lance said. "My father always made it about showing off the fancy gifts he could give us that weren't about us at all but about him impressing everyone around him. And my mother's Christmas décor, it was about having the prettiest, fanciest house around to be better than all her friends and neighbors. She'd waste thousands of dollars on decorations every year, trying to outdo everyone else. It made me sick and I promised myself I would never fall into that whole commercialism trap."

Mary grinned. "I'm glad to hear someone else isn't wasting their time and money on all those geegaws that no one needs."

"You never told me that about your childhood," Erin said to Lance. Knowing now how he saw Christmas, she wished she'd been more sensitive to those memories. Though, in all fairness, she had tried talking to him about it, but he'd always shut her down. Maybe the fact that he was willing to open up about it now meant that he was making progress with his therapy.

"I agree with you and Mary," Erin said. "That's a terrible way to have to live. I just like decorating and having pretty things around me. I decorate for all the seasons, but Christmas is the easiest and most fun. Besides, the thing I love most about all of the Christmas activities is that we do them together."

The grin left Mary's face and she looked like she was about to cry. "That's all I want from my children and grandchildren. But they never come to see me. They just send me expensive froufrous, thinking it makes up for the fact that I'm sitting here all alone."

Erin pulled up a chair and took Mary's hand. "I'm sorry your children aren't here for you. But that's why we are. You don't deserve to be alone, and we know how much more precious time and friendship is than things."

She held up the sample reindeer that one of the other ladies had made because, with her broken arm, she couldn't make one herself. "This isn't what you would call a fancy decoration. I can't even make one. But I can sit with all the ladies making their own and talk to them. Get to know them. The thing is just the excuse for getting together."

Mary nodded slowly. "I guess I hadn't thought of it like that. But I don't like making that kind of craft."

"What do you like?" Erin asked.

"Mary was just telling me about the blanket she's been knitting. I had just asked her if she could get it to show me when you walked up," Lance said.

"I've always wanted to learn how to knit," Erin said. "I'd love to see it, as well."

Mary stood, looking a little brighter than Erin had ever seen her look. "If you're serious, you come back and I'll teach you."

It sounded like a challenge, like Mary didn't think she'd really come back. But she would. Just for Mary.

As Mary walked to her room, Lance turned to Erin. "I didn't realize that about you and decorations. I guess, in the back of my head, I was always judging you, thinking you were like my mother, trying to keep up with the Joneses. But looking back, it was never a comparison for you. You were so happy, showing off whatever crafty thing you'd come up with. I never saw my mother smile and light up the way you do when it came to her Christmas decorations. Mostly she was crabby and snippy, upset because things weren't as perfect as they'd been in her mind. And the fact that your binder said 'Our Perfect Christmas,' I guess I figured that's what it was about."

The expression on his face told her that he'd legitimately been thinking about these things, trying to understand. Something he hadn't done when they were married. He'd just argue with her and tell her that all of her Christmas stuff was a waste.

Could she have been too hasty in writing him off?

He leaned forward and took her hands. "But the more I think about it, the more I realize that all of the things in your binder are about things the family can do together. That's your priority. And I stupidly missed it."

She squeezed his hands and smiled at him. "If I had understood that was why you didn't like Christmas, I would've explained to you a long time ago. I just thought you were a big old Grinch, trying to ruin everyone's fun because you didn't see practical reason behind it. Yesterday, you asked me why I could still be so happy at Christmas after everything. For me, Christmas is a reminder of how very precious my family is, and I choose to make the most of the family I have rather than mourn the family I don't."

Lance grabbed her and hugged her tightly against him. For a moment she could barely breathe, but as he loosened his grip and she hugged him back, she could hear him snuffling back tears.

She held him for a moment then released him. "I'm glad we're having this conversation now. I hope it's bringing as much healing to you as it is to me."

Lance nodded as he gestured at the hallway Mary had gone down. "That's the other reason I hate Christmas. And why I wanted to come with you today. Mary could have been my grandmother. She lived in a nursing home across town, and I remember how my mother would make a big deal of going to the mall and buying her some fancy gift. And every Christmas, we'd put her on speakerphone and she'd thank us for the gift, but I could tell she didn't really like it. Then she'd ask when we were coming to visit and my parents would always make some dumb excuse, but we hardly ever did. All my grandmother wanted for Christmas was for us to spend time with her, but I was just a kid, so I couldn't, and my parents always had better things to do. You're giving to women like Mary the very thing they want from their families but can't have."

Even though Erin had been promising herself to keep her distance, she leaned forward and gave Lance another hug. "I told you, family is what you make it. I'm sorry about your grandmother. But there are a couple dozen grandmothers and grandfathers in this room we've adopted. So be that grandson to Mary. We've been coming here for months, and you're the first person she's ever spent time talking to."

Lance shrugged. "I purposely looked for someone sitting alone. Toward the end, Grandma was difficult, and even the nurses were starting to write her off. I'm not saying Grandma was perfect. But I just wonder how much of her attitude would have been better if someone had just taken the time to care about her."

Why did he have to make this so hard? Now that she'd found a place of strength in choosing to be over Lance, he'd had to show her this beautiful piece of himself and the source of his pain in a way that gave her a deeper understanding of him. He was a good man, and the flaws she saw in him were more about the pain he'd suffered and his avoidance of facing it again.

But it wasn't her job to fix him. That was one of the things their counselor had emphasized to her over and over as Erin had kept trying to find ways to make their marriage work. In the past, she'd have seen this level of opening up to her as the kind of progress that meant they really could work things out. But now she knew it wasn't enough. Not unless he could be open with her about the grief over losing their children.

It was amazing, receiving this tenderness from Erin. He'd always loved her hugs. When Mary returned, carrying her knitting bag, there was a difference in the way she walked. The pride on her face was evident as she told them about her project. He'd admit he was glad Erin had been there, because he didn't know the first thing about knitting. However, when Mary pulled the blanket out of her bag, Lance was impressed. He didn't need to be an expert to appreciate the hard work that had gone into the delicately knitted blanket.

"It's beautiful," Erin said. "It looks so soft. May I touch it?"

Mary beamed. "Of course. I always pick the softest yarn. And, it doesn't come cheap, let me tell you. I consider it my revenge against those children of mine. They want my money? Oh, they'll get it, but I intend to spend my share before they do."

He liked Mary, and once he went back to work, he'd make a point of coming back to visit her. Maybe he could combine those visits with ones to see the boys. The drive was only a couple of hours, so he could make a day of it. He still hadn't found the courage to ask and, after the sleigh ride, he wasn't sure he wanted to get into any more personal discussions with her.

Especially considering that now, knowing Erin had been pregnant when Lily died, it was a lot harder to place the blame on her for Lily's death. So who was he supposed to blame? Himself, for being short with her, so she hadn't told him about the baby? What would that have accomplished?

Erin told him that blame was useless, but how else was he supposed to handle his feelings? In the corporate world, the person responsible for failures got fired. Why couldn't things be as simple as that?

He hadn't even intended on telling her his feelings about Christmas. He didn't like delving into that past emotional stuff. The past was past. There was nothing he could do about it, so why bother talking about it? That's the part Erin didn't seem to understand.

But Mary had been so sad and he'd thought that maybe, by sharing his experience, she wouldn't feel so alone. The Drummonds were a proud bunch, and it was important to them to keep up the appearance of being the perfect family. Hence the importance of the perfect Christmas.

With Erin, though, he'd never felt that he was a performer putting on a show. Even though talking to Mary had been about making her feel better, sharing all this old stuff with Erin, the things he'd thought pointless, had made her soften to him in a new way.

Maybe he'd been going about this all wrong.

He smiled as Erin fingered the blanket and made comments about the stitches.

"Who is the blanket for? I'm sure it will become a family heirloom for whoever it is," Erin said.

Mary gestured around the room. "Does it look like any of these old fools are having babies? I make them for a women's shelter. And for one of those teen mom programs. I figure women in those situations, they probably get all the basics, but you know, there's something about a nice, soft blanket that brings a person comfort. That is why I spare no expense on these blankets. They probably get a lot of other people's castoffs, but from me, they get the best."

The tender look on Erin's face made him smile. That had been one of the hardest things for her to get used to when they got married. She, too, had been used to castoffs and making do. But when they'd married, he'd always insisted on buying her the best. Now, looking back, he could see that she hadn't minded about whether it was new or fancy or not. That had been a carryover from his family.

"I'm sure they appreciate it," Erin said. "You're probably right about them not getting the best. Not that people always need the best, but sometimes it's nice to have a treat."

She smiled at him, like she wanted him to know that it was okay that he did give her the best, always. But as he thought about their gift conversation, he realized he'd always done exactly what he hated having been done to him. Yes, he gave her great gifts. He could see now that what she'd really wanted most from him was his time.

The last Christmas they'd been together, he'd gotten her a diamond tennis bracelet. When she'd invited him on all the crazy outings with her sisters, he'd declined, using work as his excuse. It would have been a better gift if he'd just gone with her and not worried about giving her the bracelet. She'd left it on their dresser when she'd left him.

As the day continued and they encouraged Mary to join in some of the activities, he couldn't stop thinking about how this place was his future. He'd told Ricky that he understood and accepted it. But as he looked around the drab all-purpose room that, despite all the attempts to make it look festive still carried the stale smell of a nursing home, he wondered, Was this what he was working so hard for?

Suddenly the sacrifice didn't seem worth it. As he watched Ryan run up to Erin with one of his impromptu hugs, he had to admit that he wanted something like that for himself. Not just the occasional visit with the boys, but having it permanently in his life.

So what did he fear more? Erin's rejection at him baring his soul to her or knowing that this was his future?

Pastor Roberts came to stand beside him. "It's a

good thing, what you're doing for Erin and the boys. Erin said you weren't much of a churchgoer, but I sure would love to see you join us on Sunday."

Lance tried to think of a polite way to say no. He could still hear his dad's voice in the back of his head telling him that only losers went to church because their wives wanted them to.

And then, in a moment of clarity, Lance asked himself if that was the voice he wanted to listen to. So far, everything about his time at Erin's had him questioning that voice, because everything the voice told him was wrong. He'd been desperately trying not to be the loser his father often accused him of being. But those were his father's standards. Lance didn't agree with them. Why was he beating himself up, trying so hard to live up to something he didn't want to be?

Erin's laugh carried across the room and her smile melted his insides. Could he be the man she wanted? The man who stood next to her while she laughed, the man she hugged, and the man she cuddled up to at night, telling him how much she loved him.

He'd had that once before. But he'd let his father's voice take over instead of being the man Erin had asked him to be. And maybe, this wasn't about being what anyone wanted him to be but about figuring out for himself what he wanted.

Lance turned his attention back to the pastor. "I suppose I'd be willing to give it a try. I don't have to stand up in front of the group or anything, do I?"

Pastor Roberts laughed. "No. You'll probably see some of the same people there that you see here, and I'm sure they'll all be glad to see you. I just thought that maybe, rather than sitting in the café all by yourself, you could spend some time with friends. I hope you come to know Christ, because as great as all these people are, you won't find a better one than Him. I've never believed in being a pushy salesman, trying to make you believe in something you don't. But I do enjoy building relationships."

Erin's sisters would be back before Sunday. Maybe they'd let him stay a little longer, at least to go to church, and maybe he could convince them that he could still have a relationship with the boys.

"I'll see what I can do," Lance said, trying to sound casual about it. But as the words came out of his mouth, he knew he'd find a way to be there on Sunday.

He had expected the pastor to hand him a Bible or something, but instead Pastor Roberts patted him on the back and gestured to where everyone was gathering. "I believe they're getting ready to start singing Christmas carols now. Want to join us?"

He hadn't been all that excited about the prospect of singing Christmas carols, but he'd considered it a necessary sacrifice to brighten the lives of people who need a little care and compassion. Even though Erin had been playing them nonstop in the house, this time he listened to the words.

Sure, they sang funny songs about the red-nosed reindeer, but they also sang songs about hope and love. That was exactly what Erin had been talking about earlier. Their family was missing two precious members, one he'd only barely found out about. But he still missed that little baby. He'd been struggling, trying to move on with his life and make sense of it without them. As he remembered the peace on Erin's face, he understood that while it was okay to mourn his losses, he also needed to appreciate the family he still had.

A tear slipped down his cheek and as he reached up to brush it away, Erin put her arm around him and rested her head against his shoulder the way she used to.

Funny, he hadn't been able to cry since his dad called him a loser for it all those years ago.

"I'm sorry to make you sad," she said. "I was hoping to give you happy memories of Christmas, so that maybe you didn't always look back on it with regret."

He put his arm around her and kissed the top of her head. "I don't regret spending time with you. I just don't know what to do once the holiday is over."

For a moment they stood in silence, listening to Christmas carols, their arms around one another as though they'd never separated. This was where he belonged. With Erin. Surrounded by this amazing community of people that chose to be a family to those without.

If Erin was right, and you could choose to make your own family, this is what he would choose. So how did he reconcile that with the fulfillment he also got from his business? He'd worked too hard to let it go, and with his job, he felt just as alive as he did now.

Could he find a way to have both?

Chapter Ten

Snow had been falling while they'd been at the nursing home. By the time they were done with caroling, there were several inches on the ground, with more coming down. Erin almost wished they'd left sooner, but then she would have missed out on whatever special moment had passed between her and Lance during the singing. Maybe it was too soon to hope, but something had changed in his heart, and she was glad to have somehow been a part of it.

"I guess we won't worry about whether or not it's going to be a white Christmas this year," Erin said as they arrived home, trying to focus on the practical rather than her own wishful thinking. "It was nice of Ricky to send his crew to plow our driveway. They'll probably need to do it again come morning."

"It's good how the community comes together to help one another. I don't think I've seen anything like it," Lance said. "I've always wanted to live in a place like this, but I didn't think it existed."

Erin smiled at him. "We feel the same way."

She was about to share more of what she loved about

being in Columbine Springs, but as they pulled up to the house, she could see a large tarp whipping in the breeze.

"The hay!"

Lance had no sooner put the car in Park than she was tearing off her seat belt and jumping out of the car. Into the snow. She didn't get more than a few feet before she realized her mistake.

"What are you doing?" Lance asked, catching up with her.

The boys weren't far behind. "Aunt Erin! You're not supposed to be in the snow with your walking boot," Dylan said.

Erin stopped as she stared at the tarp, whipping in the wind. "That tarp was covering ten thousand dollars' worth of hay. The snow will ruin it all."

"What do you need me to do?" Lance asked.

"We need to get the tarp back over it and minimize as much moisture getting into it as possible, in hopes that we can salvage some of it."

She turned to the boys. "Get me a big trash bag I can put over this boot, so I can help Lance."

"I'll take care of it," Lance said. "You take the boys inside where it's warm. The last thing you need to be doing on that foot is tromping through the snow and doing work."

"It's not a one-person job." Erin gave the boys her best mom stare. "Now do what I asked."

The boys looked between her and Lance like they didn't know who to listen to. "I can help Uncle Lance," Dylan said. "I'm a cowboy, and cowboys always help with the chores."

"Not in the middle of a snowstorm." Erin looked to Lance for assistance and he nodded.

"Your aunt is right. The best cowboy thing you can do right now is to take her inside and keep her warm." He looked down at Erin's foot. "And that's the best thing you can do for this ranch, too. Can you call some of your church friends or Ricky to come help me?"

As much as she hated to admit it, Lance was right. She wouldn't be as much help as she'd like to think, especially with her arm. "I'll make some calls," she said.

She led the boys into the house then pulled out her cell phone. Ricky immediately offered to send some of his hands over. It was a nice offer and she was grateful. But she also felt sick. If she'd been doing the feeding instead of Lance, maybe the tarp would have been better secured. Not that she blamed him. He was new at this whole animal care thing, and the fact that he'd even been helping her in the first place was a wonderful gift.

Maybe Lance was right about her being irresponsible. That's what he used to say about her after Lily died. When she'd been in the hospital after her accident, she'd seen that same look on his face. Even though he wouldn't have blamed her for the tarp blowing off, she should have done a better job of teaching him about it. Or maybe she should have asked Ricky or some of her friends from church to help with the animals, since Lance was so inexperienced.

But just as she started going down that road, she stopped herself. It was dangerous to play the what-if game. That was one of the things that had come between her and Lance with Lily's death.

Instead she busied herself making cookies. Since Lance and the boys had baked some earlier, the boys were familiar with what they needed to do to help her. It would be a nice treat for Lance and the men when they were done and she'd send a plate back with the guys for Ricky.

It felt good to be useful in some way. As she and the boys mixed the batter for some simple chocolate-chip cookies, the uneasiness she felt over the tarp situation disappeared. It wasn't her fault. It wasn't Lance's fault. Sometimes these things happened and that was just how life went.

By the time she got the cookies on the cookie sheet, she saw the headlights from the truck Ricky had sent over. Once again, she felt grateful for being part of such a wonderful community. As she prayed, thanking God for bringing these people into her life, she also prayed for Lance. He had Chad, but it wasn't the same as having a supportive community around him. She'd always known that he and his family weren't close, but after having talked with him during his stay, she realized just how distant they were and how deeply hurt he was by them.

Had she been wrong for giving up on him so easily? Their counselor had told her that it wasn't her job to fix him, but at times like these, she wondered if she'd done enough.

"We're going to go work on our present for Uncle Lance," Dylan said when they put the cookies in the oven.

"Okay, but don't make a mess." Erin smiled at her nephews, who raced off before she could even finish her sentence.

She had no idea what their present to him was, but they'd been hiding in Dylan's room to make it. They'd told her it was a surprise and since they didn't appear to be doing anything dangerous, she was respecting their privacy.

That got her thinking about what she would give Lance for Christmas. He'd be leaving before then, but after all he'd done for her, she wanted to do something nice for him. After their conversation at the nursing home, she could finally understand why they'd had such a disconnect over the holiday gifts they'd given one another when they were married.

As she walked into the family room, she spied Lily bear on the ground. Ryan would be hunting for it later, so she set the bear on the couch. Maybe something of Lily's, since Lance seemed to be surprised at the things she'd kept.

Erin went into her bedroom and opened the old trunk where she kept all of Lily's things. Sometimes she thought she was silly for hanging on to them, but other times she couldn't bear to get rid of them. She'd assumed Lance had kept the few things she'd left at the house, but maybe not. She certainly hadn't left anything of sentimental value, since he'd told her to take it all.

She pulled out a bag containing a bunch of quilt squares. The women at her former church had helped her make them out of Lily's old clothes to be a memory quilt. But when Erin had told them she and Lance were divorcing, the women had distanced themselves from her. One of the ladies had apologetically dropped the bag of quilt squares off at Nicole's apartment, saying they didn't feel right completing the quilt when Erin had given up on her marriage.

It had been hard, going back to church after that, but

being in Columbine Springs and its community, she didn't feel the pain of their rejection so much at seeing the quilt squares. She didn't even know why she'd hung on to them, except that they'd been made from Lily's clothes and she couldn't bring herself to part with them.

The top square was from a T-shirt that had read "Daddy's Girl," which is when Erin knew what she'd give Lance for Christmas. She'd finish the quilt for him, and even though it might bring up difficult emotions, it might also bring him healing and comfort.

The timer went off and Erin returned to the kitchen to finish readying the cookies for the men who'd been working to save their hay. Her decision about Lance's gift brought a new lightness to her heart. Even though everything in her life was far from perfect, it seemed easier now.

Whatever happened between her and Lance, it was in God's hands.

She had to trust that things would work out however they were meant to be, regardless of whether or not she and Lance ended up together.

Lance couldn't claim he'd ever had aspirations of being a cowboy before coming to Erin's ranch, but after working with Drew and Troy yesterday to try to save the hay, and hearing Dylan's constant proclamations about what cowboys do, he had to admit there was a certain appeal to the idea. He liked how the people in this community looked out for one another and came together when people were in need.

They'd told Lance that the damage to the hay was probably bad. The tarp had likely blown off shortly after the driveway had been plowed because if it had been off when Ricky's crew had come to plow, they would have fixed it. Hopefully it hadn't been off long before Erin had noticed. They wouldn't know just how bad the damage was until spring, of course. The several inches' worth of moisture would seep into the bales and cause it to mold once the weather warmed up. That would render the hay useless as feed for the animals.

Erin had said it was ten thousand dollars' worth. He'd had no idea hay cost so much money, but given the size of the haystack, he supposed he could see it. Did insurance even cover that kind of damage? Drew had said it was unlikely, causing Lance to wonder where Erin and her sisters would get the money to replace it.

Technically not his problem. But since he'd been the one feeding the animals, it had been his job to ensure the tarp was secured. He'd clearly not done a good enough job of it.

Erin had wanted him to sell the house so she could have her share of the equity to cover some of the ranch expenses. He hadn't asked her why. And, other than completely shutting her down when she'd first asked about it when he'd arrived, they hadn't talked about her reasons for needing the money. The other day she'd told him she wouldn't bother him about selling again. But now, with the hay potentially ruined, where would she get the money to replace it?

Maybe he should think about selling.

It wasn't like he needed the big house. They'd bought a giant house, saying they were going to fill it up with kids. Only now most of the rooms were empty. He'd gotten rid of a lot of the furniture, too—anything that brought up a memory had been quickly disposed of.

So why couldn't he let go of the house?

Until he'd come to Three Sisters Ranch, it was the only place he'd lived where he could remember truly being happy.

Except he wasn't happy there anymore. He wasn't happy anywhere, in general, other than being here with Erin.

He knew it was an illusion and that the only way to get back to a place with her where they could have happiness again was if he let go of…

What?

He didn't even know anymore. Though he'd basically talked himself out of holding on to some of the crazy beliefs passed on to him by his father, it didn't make what he wanted to believe in instead any clearer.

That was why he was sitting at the kitchen table, trying to make sense of the new financial reports on his laptop. They were the only things that made any sense to him.

Except they didn't.

While much of the evidence pointed to the likelihood that Janelle had been embezzling from the company, pieces of it still didn't make sense. Not just that he couldn't see Janelle doing it, but he still had no idea where any of the money had actually gone.

The boys entered the kitchen, laughing and covered in snow.

"Uncle Lance!" Ryan said, his cheeks rosy. "You should come see the snowman we made."

They'd asked him to build a snowman with them, but he'd wanted to do some more work since all his plans to do so the past couple of days had been thwarted by their fun.

Erin followed, also looking as though she'd enjoyed

herself, but, like the boys, also looking like she'd had a little too much cold.

"It's a good thing you guys came in. I think it's time for everyone to warm up. Let's have some hot cocoa," Lance said, saving the document and getting up from the computer.

"That sounds nice, thanks," Erin said, plopping into a chair.

The tone of her voice made him pause. She'd had fun, yes, but she also looked exhausted.

"I know when you were discharged, the doctor said you could return to normal activities after a few days as tolerated with your boot, but I hope you're not overdoing it," Lance said.

Erin smiled weakly. "I stayed up too late last night, working on a Christmas present. Then I tried shoveling the walk and I think I tweaked something. So, I think we'll go watch a movie and stay out of your hair."

She had to be hurting pretty badly to make such an admission.

"I know you haven't needed any lately," he said. "But you might consider taking a pain pill to take the edge off so you aren't hurting worse later."

Rather than argue, Erin sighed. "You're probably right. I know I shouldn't have tried shoveling the walk, but I was feeling so good, and I was trying to be useful. With Leah coming home tomorrow, I wanted everything to be perfect. Serves me right."

She got up and took a pill. If she was giving in that easily, she'd definitely overdone it. But at least she was willing to admit it and take care of herself now.

"I don't want to watch a movie," Dylan said. "I need to finish making my Christmas presents."

"Me, too," Ryan added, jumping up from his chair.

The boys raced off to their room, not waiting for a response. Lance started after them.

"Let them go," Erin said. "They're making Christmas gifts, and I don't want to intrude on whatever it is. They'll be fine in their room. I'll go lay on the couch with my blanket and a movie, and you can continue working on whatever it is you're working on."

He'd noticed the boys shutting themselves in their room more and more often, muttering about a surprise. It reminded him of how, when he and Erin were married, Erin would give his mother a gift she'd made herself. However, his mother had always been offended at the cheap gift Erin had given her. But now, seeing all the time and effort the boys were putting into whatever they were making, he could tell that the gift was about so much more. What was the time put into making a gift worth? Even Erin had been shut in her room at various times during his visit for whatever gifts she was making.

He'd been thinking about getting the boys each a new train, but since being in the nursing home, he was starting to wonder if that desire was still a holdover from his past. Yes, the boys would like a train, but they already had a bunch. What could he give them that meant something?

He'd have to ask Erin. He went and peeked in the living room. She had already fallen asleep with the Christmas movie on in the background. She looked beautiful, snuggled in her blanket, the Christmas lights reflecting off her face…

He wanted to do something special for her, too.

Erin would argue that his being there had been gift

enough. What she didn't realize was how much his time here had given him. He'd come, seeking peace with the past. Though he couldn't say any of it was completely resolved, things were changing in his heart and he would have a lot to discuss with his therapist when he returned home. Before, he couldn't see a way forward. He'd felt trapped, stuck. But now, while he couldn't put a finger on exactly what it was, he knew something inside him had changed for the better.

And maybe, if Erin wouldn't mind him staying an extra few days so he could go to church with them on Sunday, another one of the missing pieces in his life would fall into place.

He returned to the kitchen and got back to work, wanting to take advantage of the time he had with the house so quiet to see if he could figure out what was happening.

One of the sets of folders had a weird file name. It didn't follow the naming convention they'd agreed upon corporately. But as he dug deeper into the file and started to read the documents, he understood why.

Janelle wasn't embezzling from the company. But someone was making it look like she had been.

Accounting wasn't his strong suit—and he'd want to hire a forensic accountant to make sure—but it was clear that someone was doing a very good job of making it look like the company was not in as good a shape as it was.

Lance grabbed his phone and dialed Chad's number. Fortunately, Chad picked up on the first ring.

The boys ran into the kitchen just as Lance started explaining to Chad what he'd found.

"Boys, can you keep it down? I'm on a phone call."

"Sorry, Uncle Lance," Dylan said. "We're just getting a snack so we can finish what we were working on."

The boys each grabbed an apple then ran back to their room, slamming the door behind them.

"Sounds like you're busy there," Chad said. "Maybe we should do this another time. The business isn't going anywhere, and you'll be back from your visit soon enough."

"It's fine," Lance said. "The boys are just being boys. But I'll go into the other room where we won't be disturbed so I can go over what I found."

He grabbed his laptop and went to his bedroom. He'd still be able to hear the boys if they came out of their room, but it wouldn't be so noisy for talking to Chad.

At first, Chad didn't seem to be able to wrap his head around what was going on. But when Lance had him open the files that he'd found, Chad grew quiet. "Why would anyone frame Janelle for embezzlement? Firing her was one of the hardest things I've ever had to do."

That was one of the reasons Lance had refused to believe that Chad could have been involved with any of this. "What did the police say when you went to them?"

"Nothing," Chad said. "I know I should have, but the investors I was talking to about valuing the company to potentially buy you out said it would seriously devalue our company to have an active police investigation. I know you think I was being too heavy-handed, and just wanted you out, but I truly do care about you and I wanted you to be given a fair price."

It didn't make him feel better, knowing that Chad

hadn't gone to the police because he was afraid of an investigation hurting Lance's chances of getting a good price. "We need to. And we need to hire a forensic accountant to look deeper into what is going on and why."

"Are you accusing me?"

"No. If I thought you were behind it, I'd have just gone to the police myself. I know you wouldn't do this. But there's something fishy going on and I'm trying to make sense of it."

Chad was silent for a moment, like he was thinking. "I've had a couple of other investors approach me as well. They have the capital we need to expand."

Chad's admission made Lance's stomach hurt. They'd built the business on their own, without outside investors, and they were very proud of that fact. Lance had always thought it would make his dad proud of him, but his dad had never said anything one way or the other. But that was his dad for you. He could never bring himself to say encouraging things like, "I'm proud of you," but he was always the first to call Lance a loser.

Another reminder that living life his father's way wasn't what Lance wanted anymore. He wanted a life like Erin's, where their home was filled with laughter and encouragement, not shame.

"What did you tell them?" Lance asked.

Chad was silent for a moment and that non-answer gave Lance the information he needed.

"I've always wanted to hike Patagonia. Remember how we used to talk about doing stuff like that? All those crazy things we thought we'd end up doing when we made enough money with the business? But we're still working crazy hours and, while I enjoy the work, sometimes I think about those plans we made."

"How much did they offer you?" Lance asked.

"Not enough," Chad said. "I thought about it. Especially with the way you'd been checking out. I couldn't do it. I don't know why. They aren't happy that I've been making them wait on buying you out. But I had to give you a chance. And now, with this information, I'm wondering if maybe they have someone on the inside, deliberately setting this up, so they can buy you out at a low number and come in with the new partnership."

It was starting to sound that way to Lance. But Chad had brought up a good point. About Patagonia. About the things they'd both said they wanted to do with their lives when they built the company.

"We should look into what those investors are up to. But you bring up something else that I've realized during my time here with Erin. We made a lot of promises to ourselves when we started this business. Promises we haven't kept. What are we working so hard for? Are you going to enjoy Patagonia as much when you're seventy years old and your body is worn out from sitting behind the desk your whole life?"

"I've been thinking along those lines a lot," Chad said. "That's why the idea of bringing in investors appealed to me so much."

"If you don't need to buy me out, do you really need the capital?"

"If we want to expand as we'd been talking about," Chad answered.

The old Lance, who'd only had the business to look forward to, had been all for that plan. "What if we don't expand? Will it kill us to keep the business as it is? We do all right. Maybe if we scaled back a little, stopped working crazy hours, took actual vacations, we'd enjoy our lives."

Expressing those ideas brought a deeper peace to Lance than he'd imagined it would.

"You and Erin are getting back together, aren't you?" Chad asked.

That seemed to be the direction everyone was pushing them in. Even though it seemed obvious to everyone else, Lance still couldn't see a clear way to making things work with her.

"It's more complicated than that. We still have a lot of issues, and even if we were to work through them, I can't see her leaving this place. Our company is in Denver, which is a two-hour drive in good weather."

"You could work remote," Chad offered. "You don't need to be in the office every day."

"I can't believe you're encouraging me to get back together with Erin. You two have never gotten along."

"She and I have different priorities. For her, it's family. For me, it's my business. But since you've been divorced, you haven't been as good at what you do. I didn't realize how much better she made you. Since you've been with her, I see the old Lance."

He felt like the old Lance. He hadn't realized how much he missed him. So how could he keep it?

"So you'd be willing to work with me if I stayed here?" Lance asked.

"We'll figure it out," Chad said. "I'm just glad to have my old friend and partner back."

They talked more about the investors and how to deal with the embezzlement scheme.

When Lance and Chad were done talking, Lance pulled up the number for Janelle and called her.

"Hi Janelle. It's Lance Drummond."

For a moment he thought she was going to hang up on him. "What do you want?"

"I understand you were let go from the company."

"I didn't steal anything. But Chad wouldn't listen. Why would I steal from you guys? That place is like family to me."

The anger in her voice made him feel even worse. "I'm sorry. As you know, I've been on a leave of absence. But I saw what happened and looked into it. I think there's something deeper going on. It's clear, from what I've seen, that you couldn't have been involved. I'm sorry about what happened. Chad is, too, but he was afraid you wouldn't take his call. I know we were wrong, but it would mean a lot to us if you came back to work. We'll even give you back pay for the time you weren't working."

He heard sniffles on the other end, like she was crying. "You don't know what this means to me," she said. "No one would hire me with the accusation under which I was fired. We weren't sure how we were going to pay the mortgage, let alone pay for Christmas. Thank you for taking the time to look into it and for clearing my name. I've been praying that the truth would prevail, and it has."

They discussed details and, even though Lance had never thought of himself as much of a Scrooge, he did feel like the old man finding his redemption for giving a family their Christmas back.

It was strange, he'd just spent almost two weeks doing the kinds of Christmas things he thought he hated. But something in him had changed during that time, and now it felt good to be part of spreading Christmas cheer.

When he left his room, he figured he ought to check on the boys, who'd been quiet the whole time he'd been on the phone. Out of respect for their surprise, he knocked on the door and stood outside. "Boys? Can I come in?"

A few moments later Dylan opened the door. "Yes?"

Lance peered inside. Ryan wasn't there. "Where's your brother?"

Dylan shrugged. "I don't know. He got mad at me because I wouldn't let him use any more glitter on Aunt Erin's present. It already had way too much. So he stormed out like a baby."

Lance went into the family room where Erin was sleeping to see if Ryan had gone to snuggle up next to her, which he often did when he was feeling lonely or sad. But Erin was still sound asleep by herself.

Lance went through the entire house, looking for the little boy, but he wasn't there. The second time he passed the back door, he noticed it wasn't latched properly.

Had Ryan gone outside?

Lance went back to the boys' room. "Did your brother go outside?"

Dylan looked up from whatever he was drawing. "I don't know. Maybe. I wasn't supposed to be watching him."

No. Lance was.

And he'd gone into his room to take a call to deal with work when he should have been watching his nephews. Now Ryan was gone.

"Please, Dylan. This is important. I can't find your brother. Where might he have gone?"

Dylan shrugged. "The barn, maybe. We're not supposed to be in there without a grown-up, but sometimes a cowboy needs to be with his animals to have a good think." Then the boy snorted. "Or to pout over stupid glitter."

The barn. Of course. Ryan was always talking about the animals and constantly asking to go out there.

"Thanks," Lance told the little boy as he ran out of the room.

When he got to the barn, it was empty, save for the animals Ryan loved.

No one ever told you how easy it was for a child to disappear. He'd spent years being angry with Erin, blaming her, calling her irresponsible. And now he'd done the exact same thing.

Even though he wasn't sure God would listen to him, he closed his eyes and prayed.

Chapter Eleven

Erin was having the most wonderful dream. She and Lance were hiking in the mountains, the way they used to, and he was smiling down on her with such love that—

"Erin!" Lance was shaking her awake.

So much for her dreams.

She stretched and looked around. It was getting dark outside. She'd obviously slept a lot longer than she'd intended. As she tried adjusting herself to being awake, she caught the panicked look on Lance's face.

"What's wrong?" she asked.

"Ryan is missing."

What did he mean Ryan was missing?

"I don't understand," she said. Her head was still groggy from sleep and the pain pill. "How can he be gone?"

Lance looked stricken. "I just went to check on the boys and he's gone. I don't know what happened."

A sick feeling hit her stomach. Why had she taken the pain pill? Why had she left the boys with Lance?

He was always going on about how irresponsible she was, and now she'd just proved it again.

Wait a minute…

She didn't lose Ryan. Lance did. Not only was her nephew missing, but all those years of listening to him blaming her…

As much as she wanted to shake him and ask him how he could do such a terrible thing, they had more important things to worry about.

Erin took a deep breath and said a prayer that they'd find Ryan quickly and safely.

"When did you see him last?" Erin asked, feeling eerily calm.

Her heart was shattering in a million pieces and yet she felt a stillness unlike the suffocating panic she'd felt when she'd discovered Lily missing.

Because this time, she knew what to do.

No one should ever have to know that.

But Erin did.

And she was going to make sure that, this time, her loved one would be found safe.

Lance hadn't answered her question. She stared at him hard. "When was the last time you saw him?"

He might be a grown man, but Lance wore the expression of a little boy who'd been caught doing something wrong.

"A while ago. The boys were in their room, working on a Christmas project," he said. "When I went to check on them, Ryan was gone. Dylan said he got mad and stormed off. I can't find him anywhere in the house. I noticed the latch to the back door open, so I checked the barn, but Ryan wasn't in there, either."

Whatever grogginess she'd been feeling before was

gone now. Erin jumped up. "He knows not to go outside by himself. But if he and Dylan were fighting, he might have gone somewhere to hide. I'm surprised Ryan didn't come to me."

Usually, if the boys were fighting, they were eager to tell on each other. But if Erin had been sleeping, Ryan might not have wanted to bother her. So why hadn't Ryan gone to Lance?

"And you didn't see Ryan leave?"

Something wasn't right. Not just because Ryan was missing. Lance was being evasive. Which meant there was more to the story than he was telling.

And it could mean the difference between finding Ryan alive… No, she wasn't going to consider the alternative.

"When did you last physically lay eyes on him?" Erin asked, trying to get a better answer out of him.

Lance pulled out his phone and stared at it. "An hour ago, maybe a little longer."

By his answer, she knew that the "little" was probably not so little. He was covering up the fact that he wasn't watching them like he was supposed to.

"What were you doing? You should have had full view of the boys' room from the kitchen. You would have seen him leave."

Lance shook his head. "I went to my bedroom to take a call. The boys kept coming in the kitchen and being noisy."

"Who were you talking to?"

"Chad."

The calm she'd been feeling exploded into a million little pieces. Everything that had been wrong in their marriage…in their lives…

No wonder he hadn't been able to give her a straight answer about how long Ryan had been gone.

Erin shook her head. She couldn't deal with the betrayal now. She took a deep breath to focus on what was more important—finding her nephew.

"How long were you on the phone?"

"An hour and a half," he admitted slowly.

The words had barely gotten out of his mouth before Erin turned and called down the hall. "Dylan!"

Dylan peered out of his room. "I told Uncle Lance I don't know where he is. He's probably off hiding, being a crybaby."

"That's not how we talk about our brother," she said. "Are you sure you don't know where he might be?"

"No," Dylan said, sounding annoyed. "Now can I finish working on my picture? Ryan was getting glitter everywhere, and this is for Mr. Ricky. Real cowboys do not have glitter all over their pictures."

Erin nodded and he went back into his room.

She went through the house, searching everywhere she could think of, calling out Ryan's name. Lance trailed helplessly behind her.

"I already looked in those places," he said. "I was hoping you knew of a different hiding place he liked."

"We need to call 9-1-1," Erin said, feeling calmer than she thought possible.

"Are you sure?" Lance asked. "We only started looking."

With Lily, he'd been angry that she hadn't called sooner. She stared at him, hard. "Every minute we wait is a minute wasted," she said, pulling out her phone and dialing.

She gave the operator their information in precise

terms. Last time she'd been yelled at for being too hysterical. No one could accuse her of that, not this time. Every mistake she'd made when Lily died played in her head and she wasn't going to make them again.

A tiny voice in the back of her head reminded her that even if she'd done all those things right, it wouldn't have changed the outcome. But she had to believe that she'd learned something in all of this. The only way she could have prevented what had happened to Lily was to have not taken a nap. And with Ryan, her nap…

A sob caught in the back of her throat.

No. She wasn't going to blame herself.

How could Lance do this to them? After all the accusations, the anger, how could he have lost Ryan? But business had always been more important than anything else.

"Erin?" the operator said. "It's going to be okay. Ryan's in my son's class at preschool and I'll be praying for him. Sheriff Steele isn't far from your house. He'll be there soon. Just stay on the line with me until he gets there."

The blessing of a small town. With Lily they'd just been a statistic. Here, Ryan was a person they all knew and loved.

Keeping the phone glued to her, Erin continued looking around the room, hoping something would give her a clue as to where Ryan had gone. She spotted one of his slippers behind one of the smaller Christmas trees. She shoved the tree aside, hoping he'd just been hiding there and fallen asleep.

But no boy.

Just his slipper.

Even though Lance had said he'd already checked

the barn, Erin should check again. It was one of Ryan's favorite places, and Lance probably didn't know all of Ryan's favorite spots.

She should have known that the barn held an irresistible temptation an unhappy little boy couldn't resist. No matter how many times they'd told Ryan not to go into the barn without an adult, he always seemed to find his way there. The little boy didn't seem to understand the dangers.

Just like Lily.

A pang of grief hit her, threatening to make her collapse.

No.

She wasn't that person anymore. She'd find Ryan and he'd be okay.

She went into the mudroom and, sure enough, his boots and coat were gone. At least he'd thought that much through.

Maybe, if he was being that rational, he'd follow their other safety rules.

She pulled on the plastic cover made for her walking boot, but Lance stopped her. "Don't. I'll go. Stay on the line with the operator, so you can protect your foot."

"Like you protected my nephew? I don't think so."

He flinched and she almost regretted her words. Setting blame for Lily's disappearance and death had gotten them nowhere. Yet the pain over losing their daughter was so fresh, it was like it was happening all over again. Only it was her nephew, her sister's child, she'd been entrusted to keep safe, and she'd failed.

Tears ran down her cheeks as she tried to pray but couldn't find the words.

The operator's voice sounded smoothly through the line. "Please, Lord, be with this family."

The prayer gave Erin the strength that she needed. She appreciated the calm voice on the other end trying to provide her comfort. But she couldn't sit around and do nothing.

She handed Lance the phone. "You can keep her updated. I know his favorite places in the barn. I'm going to look for him."

Erin wrapped the tape around the top of her boot and then reached for her coat.

Lance put his hand on her arm. "Don't. Please. I know I let you down, but I'll make it right. You can't put yourself at risk, too."

She pushed his hand away. "Weren't you the one who told me that after Lily died, nothing would be right again? I can't do that to my sister."

He held the phone out to her. "Someone has to be here when the police arrive."

She gave him the coldest look she could muster. "Then you stay. And you can explain to them how you lost my nephew."

As she stepped out onto the porch, she saw the familiar truck of Margaret Cooke, their neighbor, pulling onto their driveway. As the truck screeched to a stop, her father, Frank, jumped out.

"Did you find him?"

"No. I was just headed out to the barn to look. How did you know?"

Margaret groaned. "You know Dad. He listens to the police scanner for entertainment."

Frank cackled. "And it was good, too. The McDonald brothers were shooting off bottle rockets again. Mrs. Willis was having a cow."

Despite the seriousness of the situation, Erin couldn't help smiling. The McDonald brothers were known for their pranks. She and her sisters used to joke about the boys…

A sob escaped. She'd been trying so hard to hold it all in, but what if Ryan wasn't okay? What if Ryan never got the chance to finally pull an epic prank on his brother?

Margaret patted her back gently. "It'll be okay. Dad and his buddies are on the search-and-rescue team with Pastor Roberts, and if they can find idiotic backcountry skiers who ignore avalanche warnings, then they can bring Ryan back safely, too."

As Erin nodded, she noticed Frank letting his old hunting dog, Blue, out of the back of the truck.

Ryan loved playing with Blue when they went over to the horse rescue center that Margaret ran. Maybe the site of the beloved dog would coax him out of wherever he was hiding.

"It'll be easier if you can give me something with his scent," Frank said. "Does he have a favorite toy or stuffed animal?"

Erin wiped the tears away from her face and nodded. "Lily bear. I'll go inside and get her."

She stepped through the door, where Lance was still on the phone with the operator. "Tell her that Search and Rescue is here. We'll be fine."

She ran into the boys' room, where Lily bear was sitting on Ryan's bed. A fresh wave of grief hit her when she laid eyes upon it. Dylan looked up from his coloring.

"It's bad, isn't it?"

She couldn't bring herself to answer the little boy's question. But as she picked up the bear, she took a deep breath to calm herself then turned back to him.

"It's going to be okay," she said. "Some people are coming to help look for your brother, and I need you to stay in your room and out of the way so everyone can do their job, okay?"

Dylan nodded. "I'm sorry I yelled at him for using so much glitter."

"It's not your fault. He knows he's not supposed to go outside without permission."

She gave the little boy a quick squeeze then went back outside to give the bear to Frank. He had Blue sniff the bear and then gave him the command to look for the little boy. As she watched Frank chase after his dog, she turned back to Margaret. "I should go check the barn, in case he's hiding there."

Margaret gave her shoulders a squeeze. "Blue will find him faster than you. Come on. Let's get you inside where it's warm. The cavalry has arrived."

Half a dozen vehicles, including the sheriff's SUV, pulled into the driveway. And, judging from the headlights in the distance, more were coming. They hadn't come so quickly with Lily. Certainly, living in the neatly ordered suburbs, the whole community hadn't showed up. It had taken Lance just over an hour to get home from work.

As the sheriff got out of his SUV, another familiar vehicle pulled up.

Leah.

Worse than losing her sister's child was having to force Leah to endure the bad news. Erin knew she had to tell her, but she hadn't had a moment to think about when or how.

"What's going on?" Leah asked.

Lance came up behind Erin and put his hand on her shoulder.

"What's he doing here?" Leah asked. "And what's up with your foot?"

"It's a long story," Erin said. "What are you doing home? I wasn't expecting you back until tomorrow."

"The weather report said we were in for another storm tomorrow. Rather than being stuck and potentially away from the boys another day, we caught an earlier flight," Shane said, coming to stand beside them. "Now tell us what's going on."

"Ryan's missing," Lance said. "And it's my fault."

He probably thought he was being chivalrous by taking responsibility, but chivalry wouldn't bring Ryan back.

Leah turned pale. "What do you mean, missing?"

She looked around, frantic, like she was finally taking in all the emergency vehicles in the driveway and making connections no mother should ever have to make.

Erin knew that feeling, and right about now, she knew that Leah was probably asking herself if this was a terrible nightmare and praying she'd wake up.

But it wasn't a nightmare. At least not one you woke up from. Erin put her arm around her sister.

"We're going to find him," Erin said.

A sob escaped Leah's mouth as big tears rolled down her cheeks.

The sheriff joined their group. "Why don't we all go inside and you can catch us all up? Search-and-rescue teams are already out looking for Ryan. No sense in us all standing here, freezing to death."

That was the other thing about living in a small town. Unlike in Denver, where she'd had to provide pictures and descriptions, here they all knew Ryan. Their kids had all played with the boys. To many of the searchers, Ryan wasn't a random stranger but a friend.

They went inside and the sheriff began asking questions about Ryan's disappearance.

Within minutes of them entering the house, Dylan must have heard his mom's voice because he'd come running into the room and had firmly planted himself on Leah's lap, even though he was a bit too big for it.

Leah and Shane listened as Lance explained what had happened. It killed Erin to watch the tears that occasionally flowed down her sister's cheeks. At least Leah had Shane, his arm around her, supporting her, as he occasionally murmured comforting words in his wife's ear. It was harder than Erin had imagined, watching her sister bravely try to hold herself together when she was probably falling apart on the inside. Erin knew how it felt, though when Lily had gone missing, she hadn't done such a good job keeping it together. She wished there was more she could do for her sister, but right now, they had to stay focused on finding Ryan.

When the sheriff had the information he needed, a deputy took Lance into the other room to question him further.

Erin knew the drill. She couldn't hear what was being said, but by the expression on Lance's face, she knew the deputy was probably grilling him, accusing him, without saying the words, of harming Ryan. Even though she knew in her heart that Lance would never harm a child, it also felt good for him to have a taste of what she'd been through. Not just from the investigators, but also with the accusations Lance had hurled at her.

Was he remembering?

Did he understand that this was what he'd done to her?

Shane had moved to stand near where Lance was being questioned, presumably to listen in. The anger and fear on her brother-in-law's face were evident, but Erin could tell he was doing his best to remain calm so he could find his son.

Alone with her sister, or at least as alone as they could be with people milling around, Leah turned to Erin.

"So where does Lance figure in all this? What is he doing here?"

Erin told her how Lance had come to be there. Ironic how all this started because she hadn't wanted to ruin her sister's honeymoon, and now it seemed like she'd done just that.

At some point in the conversation, someone had pressed a cup of coffee into Erin's hands, and she looked up to realize that the women from church were in the kitchen, bustling about, preparing coffee and refreshments for both the family and the search party.

When Erin got done telling her sister just how badly she'd let her down, she started crying. "I'm so sorry. You trusted me with the boys and I failed you."

Leah took the cup of coffee out of her hands then wrapped her arms around her. "It's not your fault. Ryan knew better than to go outside without permission. Besides, blame isn't going to get my son home safely."

Erin had said the same thing to Dylan, trying to keep the little boy from blaming himself. And what was she doing? Exactly the same thing she knew wouldn't get them anywhere. It had taken her months of counseling to stop accepting the blame for Lily's death. Somehow she needed to get to that place again.

Erin hugged her sister back then looked up at her. "You don't seem worried."

Leah rested her head on Erin's shoulder. "I'm scared to death. I can't help thinking of when you lost Lily and how I couldn't imagine the pain you were going through. Now that Ryan's gone, I just can't imagine what my life would be like without him."

Leah started to cry again and Erin regretted her words to her sister about not being worried. She hadn't meant to further upset her.

Shane came and sat next to his wife, putting his arm around her. "It's going to be okay. We have one of the best search-and-rescue teams in the state. Frank has even flown out to help with high-profile missing persons cases. I'm sure they'll be back with good news anytime now."

Leah pulled away from Erin and turned to her husband. "I hope so. I thought I heard Janie in the kitchen, organizing everyone to pray. We should join them."

"You go," Erin said. "I need a few moments alone."

Leah took Dylan by the hand, and the others followed her into the kitchen, but Erin remained where she was.

She'd barely started praying when she heard boots clomping on the floor. She opened her eyes and Ryan came running into her arms. "Aunt Erin, I'm okay. I found Fluffy the Second."

"Leah!" Erin shouted her sister's name, then she pulled Ryan into her arms and squeezed him tight. Tears ran down her face as she cuddled the freezing boy. He squirmed under her embrace and that's when she noticed he had something inside his coat.

"Is that a kitten?"

Ryan wiggled out of her grasp. "Yes. That's what I was trying to tell you. I heard meowing outside the door, so I opened it to see Fluffy the Second. She ran away, so I chased her, all the way to the old shed we're not supposed to play in. And I found her there, with kittens. Aren't you so happy that Fluffy the Second is alive? And we have kittens."

Fluffy the Second wasn't the only thing she was glad was still alive. And it explained a lot. Not just the cat's disappearance but also why they hadn't found Ryan quickly. She knew the shed he was talking about. It was on the far edge of the property, set away from all the outbuildings. Not only were the boys not allowed there, Ryan used to tell her that he was too scared to go there because of all the spiders. She would have never guessed that's where he'd been.

Leah entered the room, and Ryan left Erin's side to greet his mother. "Mom! I thought you weren't coming home until tomorrow. The surprise I was making for you isn't done yet. But look!"

He held up a kitten and grinned. "A kitten is an even better surprise. And you didn't even have to worry that Fluffy the Second was missing."

No, but she hadn't been spared the worry over Ryan's disappearance. And by the way Leah held her son tight, Erin knew they'd all be keeping the little boy close for a long time to come. A couple of the men entered the room, each holding a kitten. She recognized one of them as John Hansen, the local vet. "They're really cold, and the mama cat is half starved, but they should be okay," John said. "I have some food in my truck that will help them."

He smiled at Ryan. "He found the mama cat and kittens and knew they were too cold, so he put them all in his jacket and was sitting in the shed, trying to get them warm. Who knows, maybe he'll be a vet someday."

That sounded like Ryan.

She looked over at the boy, who'd escaped his mother's embrace and had turned his attention back to the kitten.

"Why didn't you come get us?" Erin asked. "We would have helped you."

"I didn't want you to be mad at me for being in the shed." He looked at all the people milling around the house. "I'm in big trouble, aren't I?"

She'd have liked to have said yes, given all the trouble he'd caused, but she was so grateful to have him safely home that she shook her head. "You know the rules. But I'd like to think that you learned your lesson. Did you?"

Ryan nodded. "The police are here and everything. They're not going to arrest Uncle Lance, are they? The mean one who sometimes comes to our school looked like he was giving him a talking to." Then Ryan's eyes widened. "They're not coming to arrest me, are they? I know I broke the rules, but I was just so happy to see Fluffy the Second—"

Dylan ran into the room and tackled his little brother into a big hug. "You're alive. I'm sorry I yelled at you for glitter. You can put as much glitter on stuff as you want. Just don't ever get missing again."

Ryan hugged Dylan back then pulled away. "I didn't run away because of you. I found Fluffy the Second. She didn't get eaten by a coyote. She had babies."

"Cool," Dylan said. "Did you see Mom and Dad came home early? Now that we found you, we can see what presents they brought us."

A scared expression filled Ryan's face. "You guys didn't come home early because of me, did you? Uncle Lance came to stay with us so Auntie Erin wouldn't ruin your honeymoon. I didn't ruin your honeymoon, did I?" Tears ran down his cheeks. "I just wanted to help Fluffy the Second. I didn't mean to cause so much trouble."

Leah held her arms out to her son. "We came home early because of the weather. You didn't ruin our honeymoon. But we do need to have a talk about following the rules from now on. All these people came because we were worried about you."

Erin gave her nephew a little nudge. She might have been worried sick, but so had the little boy's mother. And she needed to hold her baby. Ryan sighed. "The police are here to arrest me, aren't they? I guess I'm going to jail."

"You're not going to jail," Leah told him as he finally entered her embrace. "And no one is getting arrested. When your aunt and uncle couldn't find you, they thought that something bad had happened to you. So they called the police to help. That's why you can't go outside without permission."

Lance entered the room, looking exhausted. "He's okay," he said with a catch in his voice.

Now that Ryan was safe, all the anger Erin had been feeling toward Lance over how he'd treated her when she'd lost Lily came bubbling up. How could he have treated her like that and then lost Ryan because he'd been too focused on work?

Ryan might get a talking to about not running off, but Lance was going to get a talking to of his own.

Before she could ask Lance if she could speak with him privately, Leah cleared her throat and gave Ryan a little nudge. "Go give your uncle Lance a hug. He was really scared for you."

Ryan ran to his uncle and threw his arms around him. Lance scooped him up and held him close.

Erin had thought she'd forgiven Lance when he'd first come here, but as she watched him embrace Ryan, she couldn't help feeling a new level of bitterness and resentment.

Yes, everything had turned out all right in the end, but it made his previous treatment of her all the more inexcusable. Now that she didn't have to focus her attention on finding Ryan, she could allow herself to feel the anger she'd been pushing away.

When the police had been questioning them, Shane had been comforting Leah, not accusing her along with them. And even Leah, who had more to lose than Erin, hadn't hurled insults at Erin for being irresponsible and losing her son. Yes, she'd been upset, and she'd cried, but she hadn't once told Erin that she was a bad person because she'd entrusted Lance with Ryan, and Lance had lost him. In fact, Leah hadn't even hurled nasty accusations at Lance, who had been at fault. Leah had even encouraged Ryan to go hug him.

The contrast was more heartbreaking than Erin would have imagined.

At least Leah was home early, which meant Lance could leave and finally get out of her hair forever. She didn't even care about the house anymore. He could sell it when he was ready, but as far as she was concerned, this would be the last time she'd ever see him.

Erin was done with any thoughts of getting back together with Lance.

Chapter Twelve

Having Ryan in his arms was the greatest gift Lance could have asked for. He wasn't sure how he would have been able to live with himself if something bad had happened to the little boy. As he looked over at the tears in Erin's eyes, all he could think about was what a horrible thing he'd done to her by blaming her for Lily's death.

The guilt he felt over Ryan's disappearance had been unbearable. Even though this time it had been a happy ending, he was still chastising himself for not doing a better job of watching the boys. He'd always known that Erin had felt terrible over what had happened to Lily. Now he could understand what an unbearable weight it must have been.

"Don't cry, Uncle Lance," Ryan said. "I'm sorry for making you worry. If it will make you feel better, I'll let you have one of our kittens."

Lance still held on to the little boy and Ryan seemed to understand that Lance needed this because he didn't wiggle free. He just rested his head on Lance's shoulder. "I love you, Uncle Lance," Ryan said.

Lance gave Ryan a squeeze then set him down. "Once the vet says the kittens can be away from the mama, I would be honored to have one of them," he said.

It was a dumb thing to say, considering he'd always said he didn't want pets, and even though Erin had often begged him for one, he'd flatly refused. But it seemed like the little boy's offer of a kitten was his way of saying that he forgave Lance, even though Lance was still not sure he forgave himself.

Lance turned and went into the kitchen, where all the people who'd helped search for Ryan were drinking coffee and eating cookies.

Everyone greeted him warmly, like he hadn't just lost his nephew and created such a big mess. One of the ladies handed him a cup of coffee. "This should warm you up."

The deputy who'd been grilling him for the past hour came in through the back door, and he, too, was given a cup of coffee.

He took the coffee, walked up to Lance and held out his hand. "No hard feelings. I know this is probably upsetting for you, but I was just doing my job."

Lance shook his hand and stared at the man. "I get it. You read stories in the news about all the sickos out there."

The deputy nodded. "We don't get too many missing persons cases out here, except the hikers and backpackers who go off trail. I'm glad we found Ryan safely. He's a good kid and you shouldn't blame yourself for what happened. My mom tells a story about when I was little boy. I disappeared while playing hide-and-seek with my brother. I hid in a clothes hamper and covered myself with all the clothes so he wouldn't find me. Then I fell asleep. Same situation as here. All the neighbors, all the police, and my mother were just sick. I woke up from my nap, crawled out of the hamper and was mad that my brother hadn't found me yet."

Erin's friend Janie held a plate of cookies out to them. "It's true. You think that you're going to be the perfect parent and do everything right. But kids have a mind of their own and things like this happen. We all just need to be grateful that Ryan is okay."

Easy for her to say. Her daughter hadn't disappeared and died. The bitter thought didn't hurt the way it used to and wasn't charged with anger toward Erin.

So who was he supposed to be angry at?

Lance took a cookie and thanked Janie then left the kitchen. Ricky was standing in the entryway with Pastor Roberts.

"So glad our little Ryan is safe," Ricky said. "That kid is something else, I tell you."

"He might be fine now, but I also lost him," Lance said. "What if things had turned out differently?"

Pastor Roberts nodded. "It doesn't do any good to place blame. Everyone has been telling you that no one can keep their eyes on their kids 24/7. So let go, forgive yourself, because it doesn't do any good to dwell on the what-ifs."

Maybe that was true. But Lance wasn't sure he knew how. He'd carried the weight of guilt and anger around for so long, he wasn't sure how to change it.

"I was supposed to come here to make peace with Erin over our divorce and daughter's death. Today I realized just how wrong I'd been in treating her. I'm a horrible person. No wonder she left me."

Ricky glared at him. “Stop that right now. You’re both hurting, and it’s no wonder. Losing a child is the toughest thing that can happen to a person. When my boy died, I was mad at the world, but mostly at myself because I’d been the one to push him away. I’ve lived a lot of years carrying around bitterness and anger, and you know what? It didn’t bring him back. It didn’t bring my wife back after she died. Rather than focusing on all the bad things you did, maybe you should talk to Erin and find out how you can move forward.”

Pastor Roberts nodded. “We look at a lot of things and say we don’t have a choice. But the one thing we can always choose is whether or not we bury ourselves in the past or move forward in the future. Maybe the peace you needed to make was to understand the wrongs so you could make it right. God doesn’t ask us to dwell in our mistakes. He forgives and wipes the slate clean. If you ask Him for forgiveness, He’ll do just that. So give Him your sins, your feelings of everything you’ve done wrong, and all this pain you’re carrying around.”

They made it sound so simple, but he could still picture the pain in Erin’s eyes as he’d hurled accusation after accusation at her. How did you forget hurting someone you loved?

She’d even been right about putting his business before family. And here he was, doing it again.

It had almost cost him his nephew.

True, Ryan’s life hadn’t actually been in danger. But what if something had happened to him out there?

“Do you mind if I pray for you?” Pastor Roberts asked.

Lance closed his eyes and, as the pastor prayed,

could feel the peace washing over him. Erin used to tell him about feeling peaceful when she prayed, but Lance had never felt the same. Now, he understood.

The love and acceptance he felt from all these people was a reflection of the love and acceptance that came from God. Someone had called Ricky and a couple of friends from church, and almost everyone he knew from the church activities he'd attended was there. These people had literally dropped everything in their lives to help look for Ryan. And now that Ryan had been found safe, they were all in the kitchen and family room, celebrating.

Erin used to tell him that God's love was so much more perfect than that of people. He'd always seen God as that stern father, mirroring his own. He'd never known love from his father, never known acceptance. Just the constant striving for perfection. As he looked over at Erin talking to her sister, he knew that she had never asked that of him.

When Pastor Roberts said, "Amen," Lance opened his eyes and looked at the pastor. "Thank you for that prayer, and for accepting a man who had absolutely no interest in church. Maybe church, and God, isn't what I thought it was. I'm looking forward to joining you on Sunday."

He realized he hadn't talked with Erin about staying longer, so he added, "That is, if I'm still here. I'd like to be, but I'm not sure how long the family will let me stay."

"You can stay at my house if you want," Pastor Roberts said. "We have plenty of room, and you're always welcome."

The hospitality warmed him. Feeling bolstered by

his newfound faith, Lance went over to Erin. "I just spoke with the pastor, and we prayed. I think I finally understand everything you've always told me about faith. I do need God in my life, and if it wasn't for you not giving up on me, I don't think I could say the same."

The coldness in her eyes burned him worse than the dry ice he sometimes got for camping.

"I'm glad for you," she said slowly. "Perhaps God will give you whatever peace you were looking for. Because it's not here. You did your job. You took care of me until my sister got here. Your services are no longer needed."

This wasn't the Erin he knew and loved.

Leah came to stand beside her sister and put her arm around her. "Thank you for taking care of the boys so Shane and I could have a honeymoon," she said. "We don't blame you for what happened with Ryan. It could have been anyone."

Even though others had said the same thing to him, he could see the anger burning in Erin's eyes. She blamed him.

How could he fault her? When Lily died, Lance had hurled accusations at her and made sure, every time he saw her, that he held her responsible for their daughter's death. He'd already come to the conclusion that it wasn't her fault. But he hadn't had the opportunity to talk to her about it.

No, that wasn't true. They'd had plenty of opportunity to talk. But Lance had always found something better to do and, following his old patterns, hadn't told Erin how he was feeling.

He excused himself and headed toward the family room, where it was quieter. As he left the room, he saw Janie and Margaret go over to Erin and embrace her. Watching the hugs made him realize that it should have been him offering her the comfort. Then he remembered how, when Lily died, he'd refused Erin's comfort, telling her she didn't have the right when it was her fault their daughter was gone.

When Erin was in the hospital, she'd told him that she didn't think he was a monster. But now, knowing what he'd put her through, knowing the agony of what she'd had to feel, only on a smaller scale, he couldn't see himself as anything but one.

He'd thought her wrong for leaving him. He thought her cold for trying to move on.

But now he understood.

She'd been hurting, too. Devastated. And he'd only piled on more pain.

His counselor had told him he needed to make peace with Erin over the divorce and the loss of Lily. But she was wrong. The peace that had needed to be made was with himself. To deal with his grief. His pain. It had been easier when he'd had someone to blame. Because now, understanding that Erin had been sleeping because she was pregnant and how unsympathetic he'd been to her, he could see where he'd been at fault, too.

However even in reassigning that blame, it didn't change the fact that Lily was dead. And so was their unborn baby, a child he'd never even had the chance to love.

A wave of grief hit him hard in the stomach, nearly knocking the breath out of him.

So much lost and he'd pushed away the one person who would understand.

He looked over his shoulder to see Erin warmly hugging another person who'd come to help her. In her new home, her new life, she had a whole community of people who were there for her. Unlike him. He turned to his job for comfort instead of his wife. Even before Lily, he'd put his company before the people he'd said he loved.

Erin had told him that she hoped God would give him the peace he needed. And he prayed that she was right. She'd made it clear she didn't want him there anymore, and he was grateful that the pastor had offered him a place to stay. He'd spend the night there, and in the morning, he'd go back home, call his counselor and maybe, with her help and the assistance of God, he could finally come to terms with the monster he'd been and the man he wanted to be.

As he turned to leave, he nearly ran into Shane.

"Hey," Shane said. "Now that the dust is settling, we should officially meet. I'm Shane Jackson, Leah's husband, and the boys' father. I appreciate the way you helped out with Erin and the boys." Though Shane held his hand out to him, Lance didn't take it.

"You forgot the part about me losing your son," Lance said.

Shane nodded slowly but didn't withdraw his hand. "It happens to the best of us," he said slowly. "Did Erin tell you about the first time we met?"

Lance shook his head.

Shane grinned. "Well, shake my hand so folks don't think you have a grudge against me, then we'll have a cup of coffee and I'll tell you all about how Leah lost the boys and I helped her keep them safe."

Lance reached out, shook Shane's hand and then followed him into the kitchen.

When people had heard about how Lily had died, everyone had come to him with their stories of how easy it was to lose a child. He'd dismissed them all because their child hadn't died. Seeing the compassion and forgiveness in Shane's eyes, he realized they'd all just been trying to help him with his grief.

They hadn't had this kind of community when Lily died. Sure, there were people from their church, but he hadn't had relationships with any of them. He barely knew these people, but he'd like to think that the many people milling around the farmhouse were all friends. He'd never thought that any of the people in their old church had cared about him personally. But here, every smile, every casual squeeze, was about a community that cared. They wanted to provide comfort and ease his crushing guilt over having lost Ryan.

Shane told the story of meeting these three women who knew nothing about ranching, and how he'd had to teach them about keeping the boys safe in this environment.

There were so many dangers and risks in raising a child. At some point you had to recognize that you'd done the best that you could and leave the rest in God's hands.

Lance had done neither.

Worse, he'd resented Erin for trying to do both. He'd expected a level of perfection he hadn't realized until now was impossible.

So what now?

He loved Erin. That he couldn't deny. But he'd wronged her on such a deep level that until he found peace inside himself, he wouldn't be able to make it right.

Out of the corner of his eye, he saw the pastor making his goodbyes.

"I have to go," Lance told Shane.

Fortunately he didn't have much by way of belongings, just the few things he'd picked up for his temporary stay.

"You don't have to go," Shane said. "No one is mad at you."

Erin was. And she had the right to be. So how did he fix it? He didn't know, but until he figured it out, he'd give Erin her space.

"Thank you all the same," he said. "But the pastor invited me to stay at his house, and I think, given the circumstances, it's best I do so."

Shane didn't argue as he let him go. He'd probably heard enough about Lance and Erin's divorce to know just how badly Lance had messed things up.

Maybe someday Lance could find a way to make them right.

Later that night, Erin was curled on the couch with her sister, a fire crackling in the fireplace. With all the excitement over Ryan's disappearance, they'd decided to go ahead and spend the night there, rather than go back to Shane's house. Even though Erin knew that Leah would eventually have to make her home with Shane, she wasn't sure she could handle being alone tonight.

Not with the memories and fresh waves of grief that had been hitting her all day.

"You can't blame Lance," Leah said. "Everything turned out fine. Besides, we all know how easy it is to lose track of the boys."

It didn't make the pain in Erin's heart any better. "In theory, I know that to be true. But I keep replaying all the horrible things he said to me when Lily died."

"Did you deserve it?"

Erin sat straighter. "Of course not. And now that I'm not panicking about Ryan, all of the logical reasons why it was just a dumb accident keep going through my head."

Erin sighed. "But then I remember that the whole reason this happened was that Lance was on the phone with Chad. I thought he'd changed. I thought he'd finally learned that family was more important than business."

Her sister put her arm around her. "I'm sorry. I know how hurtful it was to you when you were married."

Erin shrugged. "I guess it wasn't meant to be. A part of me still loved Lance, and I had this crazy hope that we'd get back together. But now I know that we can't." She reached for the cup of tea she had on the side table and took a sip. "Business comes first with him. I won't let our family be second."

She paused, knowing that wasn't all of it. "That, and I'm not sure I can forgive him for how he treated me when Lily died."

Leah nodded slowly. "Because he blamed you?"

"It's more than that. I saw how Shane was there for you when Ryan was missing. And how, when I opened the door for you to blame me for Ryan's disappearance, you comforted me instead."

"Why wouldn't I? We were both fearful and grieving. I know you, and I know that you will always put the boys' best interests first."

Her sister's words added to the pain in Erin's heart. "But Lance didn't. Instead of grieving with me, and working through things together, he pushed me away and blamed me. Like he didn't know me at all."

Maybe they both hadn't known each other. After all, she'd learned of his reasons to dislike Christmas only recently. He'd never opened up to her about his feelings—about the holiday, about Lily's death, about anything important.

If they couldn't talk about things that were important, and he hadn't trusted in her character, or her love for their daughter, what did they have?

It didn't matter. They were, and would remain, divorced.

Erin looked around at the disarray in the family room.

"I'm tired of talking about it," Erin said. "It's over. Let's get on with our lives and what's important. Like salvaging what we can of Christmas."

Many of her decorations had been knocked down or moved to set up for rescue operations. Even though the ladies from church had cleaned the kitchen before they'd left, many of the decorations had been torn or were dirty. They'd had to throw away many of the things she and the boys had made. The kitchen tree had been moved to the porch and, at some point while it was on the porch, someone had knocked it over. The same with all the other trees in the house. Even the boys' tree had been disheveled because Dylan had gotten upset when he'd realized his brother was truly gone and he reacted out of anger.

The only tree unscathed by Ryan's disappearance was the one in Erin's room. Where it had once brought her joy, it now only made her feel profoundly sad.

She thought that with the perfect Christmas, she and her family would make new memories to ease the pain of the bad. Not that any of it could be replaced, but she'd thought that adding happy memories would make it easier.

Now it felt like a shadow had been cast over the new things she'd try to create.

She gestured at the mess, not knowing where to start. "All this work, and it's destroyed."

"We can fix it," Leah said. "I'll get a trash bag, and we can start fresh tomorrow."

Start fresh? It had taken her weeks to do this much. They'd never be ready in time for Christmas.

"I ruined Christmas," Erin said, trying not to cry. "I was trying so hard to make the perfect Christmas so we could finally have the holiday we'd always dreamed of, but now it's ruined."

Leah took the cup of tea out of Erin's hands and set it down before hugging her. "How can you even say that? We're all together. We're happy. We're healthy. Ryan was found safe. As long as we have each other, that's all that matters."

In her heart Erin knew it was true. The idea that everything had to be pretty and perfect was precisely why Lance had said he hated Christmas. But it wasn't just that.

Erin picked up a mangled snowflake. "We worked

so hard for everything to be nice. I wanted the boys to have wonderful memories, unlike ours."

Leah hugged her again. "They do have wonderful memories. They can't stop talking about all the fun they had with you and Uncle Lance."

For Erin, it would be just one more bitter memory of the past. How her heart had been broken once and truly for all.

Leah gave Erin another quick squeeze. "I hate to bring this up now, but the boys have been asking if Lance can come for Christmas. Shane and I were talking. They really love him. We'd like to invite him to spend time with the boys, but we don't want to cause you pain."

Erin figured this would happen. The boys loved Lance. Her issues with him were her issues, not theirs.

"It's fine," Erin said. "Despite my anger at him for focusing on work when he should've been watching them, he's really good with them. I don't want to deprive them of someone they love. I'll be okay."

Somehow she knew she would be. Yes, it would hurt seeing him, but at least now she wasn't holding on to the ridiculous hope that she and Lance would be together again. He couldn't be the man she wanted and that was okay. She had to believe that God had someone better for her. It was the same thing she'd been telling herself all along, but she finally believed it.

"At least I saved the big tree for us all to do together," Erin finally said.

"Yes," Leah said. "And Shane is rigging up something so you can go with us to get it. We're still going to make wonderful memories."

Her sister's enthusiasm made Erin feel a little better.

This time when she looked around the room, she didn't see all the mess and wasted effort. Instead she remembered the boys laughing and, with a pang, being here with Lance.

Yes, the Christmas she'd hoped to have was ruined. But maybe now the wound of her broken marriage would finally heal.

Even though she didn't owe Lance anything, she'd continue working on the quilt, and as she sewed the pieces together, she'd pray for healing, for all that she'd lost, and trust that God would bring peace to her heart.

Chapter Thirteen

Christmas Eve, Lance arrived at the ranch house feeling more nervous than a boy picking up a girl for their first date.

That was ridiculous, considering this was not a date.

Leah had invited him to spend the evening with their family, which he'd accepted, but she'd been cagey about how Erin felt. Now he was wondering if he shouldn't have first gotten Erin's explicit permission.

"Sorry I'm late," he said as Leah ushered him in. "I had to make a stop at the nursing home to see my friend Mary, and it took longer than I thought."

"It's fine," she said, smiling. "We only just got here, and Nicole and Fernando haven't arrived yet."

Leah hugged him with more warmth than he expected, despite the fact that he was there on her invitation. He handed her the bag of gifts he'd brought, but as he did so, he removed the box for Erin.

"I don't know how you want to do presents, but I have a few things for everyone." He held up the box he'd pulled out. "But I'd like to give this to Erin privately."

No sooner had he spoken than Dylan and Ryan ran into the room and wrapped their arms around him.

"Uncle Lance!" The boys immediately started chattering at him, so fast, he couldn't keep up.

Shane stepped into the room. "Boys, give Lance his space. You still have chores to finish. You can catch up with him in a little while."

The boys ran back out of the room and Shane shook his head. "They have Christmas fever. But I promised Erin we'd bring in some more firewood, and it's getting dark."

Lance nodded. "She probably says she's fine to do it, but she still needs help."

Shane grinned. "Pretty much."

Erin joined them. "Oh, stop. I'm not that bad."

He shouldn't still be so affected by the sight of her. It had only been a week, but it was enough to realize how much he missed—and still loved—her.

He just prayed it wasn't too late.

"Do you think we could speak privately for a moment?" he asked.

Erin looked over at Leah, who nodded.

"We can go to my room," Erin said.

He followed her, feeling Shane's and Leah's eyes on him. He felt like a boy sneaking up to a girl's room, even though he'd been to Erin's room before and they'd once been married. But he'd never felt as though so much was at stake before. Even when he'd asked her to marry him, he'd known she was going to say yes.

But now he was about to bare his heart and he wasn't sure how she'd receive it. The last time they'd spoken, she had been angry with him, and rightfully so.

Would she be willing to forgive him?

When she closed the door behind them, he said, "Thank you for letting me come. I know Leah would've gotten your approval before inviting me, but I wasn't sure how grudging it would be."

Erin shrugged. "The boys love you. I can act like an adult for their sakes."

"You're still mad at me?"

She looked like he'd just asked her a ridiculous question. "After all the hurtful things you said to me after Lily died? And then for you to do the same thing?"

He watched as she squeezed her eyes shut.

She stared at him again. "I know Ryan didn't die. But with Lily, I was pregnant, and with Ryan you were obsessed with work. Again."

Her accusation hit him square in the gut. He deserved her words, but he hadn't expected them to hurt so much.

"You're absolutely right. I behaved abominably toward you after Lily died. I've been regretting my actions, even more so after learning about the baby. I should have told you that, even before Ryan disappeared, but I kept chickening out about sharing my feelings with you."

Her face softened a little, but he knew he was nowhere near close to winning her over.

"I spent the first night after I left at the pastor's house, and he and I sat up for a while, talking about all this. I told him a lot of things, and they were all things I should have told you to begin with. So the next day, I got in my car and drove home. I had a few sessions with my counselor to sort things out, but I know that the person I've needed to talk to the most was you."

Both his counselor and the pastor had warned him

that he could open his heart to her and she still might reject him. But he also knew that he owed it to Erin to take that risk. She needed to hear what he had to say.

"I will never be able to find the words to tell you how deeply sorry I am for all of the horrible things I said to you when Lily died. I was wrong to blame you, and even more wrong not to turn to you for comfort… Our little girl died, and what you needed most was for your husband to come alongside you and love you and figure out a way to move on together. You shouldn't have been alone when you lost the baby. I should have been there, holding your hand, and together, we would have faced the future."

Tears rolled down Erin's face as she nodded. None of this was news to her. Because it was what she had told him all along. But for the first time, he was confirming it.

"I can't go back and do what I should have done. But I can do better in the future. I once told you that I couldn't be the man you wanted me to be. But I'd like to try." Tears stung the backs of his eyes and he couldn't ever remember being this vulnerable to her. Vulnerability made a man weak, according to his father, but he now knew that his father didn't have the character Lance wanted to emulate.

Lance held his hand out to Erin. "I miss Lily. Sometimes I think about what she would've been like, or I see a little girl playing in the park, and it hurts so much to know that our daughter will never get to do any of that. I wonder about the baby we lost and I mourn what could have been. I should have shared all this with you. But I was too busy trying to make my father proud, when I should have been more focused on loving my wife."

The tears running down Erin's face as she took his hand gave him hope.

"I miss them, too," she said. "And I felt all alone in my pain."

"You're not alone. I'm sorry for not sharing it with you. I haven't shared a lot of things with you, and I can see where I've let you down as a husband."

As she nodded, the ache in his heart grew. Maybe it was too much to expect that a simple conversation could fix everything between them, but surely it was a start.

He handed her the box. "I wanted to give this to you privately because it's a symbol of my commitment to listening to you and working on meeting your needs."

She opened the box and he saw the tears that sprang to her eyes as she scanned the documents within. "It's an offer on our house."

He nodded. "Maybe I should have asked you before putting it on the market. But you'd been asking me to sell for so long, I figured it would be okay. So, take a look at the offer and, if you like it, we'll sign. The house will be sold and we can start our next chapter."

Then he took a deep breath. "What that chapter looks like is up to you. When I was taking care of you, you asked if we could start again. But in my pride and anger, and lack of understanding, I didn't give you the answer you were hoping for… I hope it's not too late. I never stopped loving you, and I think that's why I was so angry with you at times. I didn't want to love you, but I couldn't help myself. And unlike the offer on this house, you can have all the time you want to think about it."

"Do you have a pen?"

It wasn't the response he'd expected, but at this point he'd take what he could get. "In the box."

She signed the papers on all the lines indicated then she noticed the final sheet.

"What's this transfer of an extra ten thousand dollars to me after closing? That wasn't part of our divorce."

He shrugged. "You wanted the money from the sale of the house to put back into the ranch. My carelessness caused damage to your hay. Even though Shane says that we won't know until the spring how much was damaged, I want to pay for it. It's a sign of my commitment to your success on Three Sisters Ranch. I want to help you and your sisters build it to be everything you've ever dreamed of."

She looked incredulous and he didn't blame her. "I haven't done much in the way of supporting you in your dreams. I've always been too focused on building my business to listen to you and what you want. I know this doesn't fix everything that's wrong between us, but I hope it's a start."

She picked up the papers and clutched them to her chest. "This means a lot. You're right, it doesn't fix everything. But you've shared more with me about your feelings in these past few minutes we've been talking than I think you did in our entire marriage. I don't know if we have a future. But this is a good beginning."

Though he hadn't been expecting her to jump up and down and ask him to marry her right away, the fact that she was open to giving him a chance filled him with hope.

"You should also know that Chad and I decided to sell the business. As we were looking at the company and seeing the direction it was taking for the future, we both realized that we were building it for dreams that would be impossible to reach if we kept up the pace we've been going at. I thought I was providing for my family. But I lost that family because I was too focused on my business. Chad wanted to travel and do more extreme sports, but he couldn't because he was always stuck in the office."

Erin nodded slowly, like she wasn't sure how she was supposed to respond, so Lance continued.

"When I took my leave of absence, Chad spoke to a number of companies to find out what he could get for my share in case he needed to buy me out. One of them was dishonest, and tried to undermine us, which is what I was working on uncovering when Ryan went missing. It doesn't excuse my actions in putting business before family, but I did save a number of jobs and I kept a lot of Christmases from being ruined." He grinned at her. "Kind of like that Scrooge cartoon character in that movie based on *A Christmas Carol* you and Ryan like to watch, except I wasn't the one who ruined their Christmas. But it feels good to know I made it right. Anyway, one of the other companies heard about what was going on, and they came in with a fair offer that would give Chad and me the opportunity to do the things we wanted with our lives."

Erin looked confused. "So what is the next chapter of your life?"

Lance shrugged. "I still need to talk to Ricky. I'll

get him preferred pricing before the deal closes, so that should make him happy. And then, if you won't mind having me around, I'll see what he has in mind for having someone take his guests up into the mountains. I just figured it might be easier to win you back if I lived locally. Besides, I'm going to start going to church here, too."

He knew it was a lot for her to take in. Lance was making a huge life change, and he'd done it all without consulting her. Even though one of the problems in their marriage had been them not talking about things, he also knew that the decisions he'd made were ones he'd needed to make on his own, to know what he wanted out of life, before he could ask Erin to share it with him again.

He just prayed that she could see the effort he'd made and his honest desire to make things right for both of them. And, if he'd hurt her too badly for her to move forward with him, he'd have the strength to do so alone.

It was all so overwhelming, hearing about the progress Lance had made. He wasn't just paying lip service to the longings of her heart, he was showing her that he was fully committed to doing things right this time.

"You're really selling the company?" she asked, not sure she could believe the words.

"I didn't think to print everything out for you, but if you want, I can pull up the email on my phone with the details. Being here, I've realized that I can build the biggest, most successful outdoor gear company in the world, but what does it matter if I spend the rest of my life alone?"

She set the house papers down on her bed and held her arms out to him. "I told Leah the other day that I thought I'd ruined Christmas. She reminded me that we were all together, so despite everything that has gone wrong, we can still have the best Christmas ever. I know we have things to work out, but I am willing to give us another chance."

As Lance embraced her, she breathed in his warmth and felt comfort in his arms. This was all she had wanted when Lily had died. When she'd lost Noel. And, yes, even when Ryan had gone missing. Together they were stronger and maybe now they could finally come to a place of healing.

She gave him a final squeeze then stepped away. "I'm sure the boys are eager to open presents. But after they leave, I'd like to continue this conversation. I never stopped loving you, either, but there were definitely moments when I was so upset with you that I wanted to. But now I finally believe that we have a chance after all."

Lance's smile warmed her heart and when he stepped in toward her, she knew he intended to kiss her.

It was a soft, tender kiss. One that spoke of the promise of a future where they would both share each other's hearts.

As Lance pulled away, he looked almost like an embarrassed schoolboy. "I hope I didn't get too carried away," he said.

She smiled and reached for his hand. "I think it was just right. Now let's go join my family."

When they entered the family room, Erin was surprised at the pile of packages surrounding the tree.

"You were supposed to be on a honeymoon, not a shopping spree," she said, looking at Leah.

Leah and Shane glanced at each other and then laughed. "We didn't exactly have a lot of time for shopping on our honeymoon. A lot of these are things from the boys. They made everyone a gift this year."

Erin nodded. She'd seen their industry while their parents had been gone.

Nicole and Fernando joined the group and Erin introduced Lance to Fernando.

Nicole gave Lance a bit of a side eye. "I thought you were mad at him. He's holding you a little too tightly for someone you hate."

Erin took a deep breath as she looked at her sisters and their husbands, who all seemed so happy together. "Lance and I had a chance to talk and, while we definitely need to sit down and sort through things, we decided to give our relationship another try."

Though Nicole looked a bit surprised, Leah smiled knowingly. Erin had had a feeling that her sister hadn't just invited Lance for the boys' sake, but because she'd known that, deep down, Erin's broken heart was just another sign of her love for Lance.

"Is it present time yet?" Dylan asked. "Because I've been waiting to give out mine for a long time."

Shane grinned. "All right, then. Why don't you go ahead and start?"

Dylan struggled with one of the larger boxes that he brought over to Lance.

"This is a real important gift. It is a sign of my respect and love for you as a fellow cowboy."

Tears filled Erin's eyes. Even before Lance opened it, Dylan's speech told her exactly what it was. Leah had told her Shane had given Dylan a speech about being a cowboy when he'd given Dylan his cowboy hat.

As Lance pulled the hat out of the box, he looked over at Dylan. "Thank you. It's a real honor. I'll wear it with pride." He set it on his head then turned his attention back to Dylan. "How were you able to afford such a nice gift?"

Dylan squared his shoulders and stood proudly. "When Mom and Dad got back from their honeymoon, I told them what I wanted to give you, and that I needed to earn the money for it. So Dad gave me some extra chores, and I did them, because a real cowboy earns his keep."

Lance held his arms out to Dylan. "I hope cowboys hug, because an extra-special gift deserves an extra-special big hug."

Could her heart melt any more? Dylan ran into his arms and Lance gave him a tight squeeze.

As everyone continued opening gifts, Erin noticed Lance withdrawing slightly.

"Are you okay? Is this too much?"

He shook his head. "No. I was just thinking how much I once hated Christmas. But I think it just may be my favorite holiday now."

His voice cracked slightly and she knew that later tonight they'd sit by the fire and he'd share more of his heart. And, hopefully, a few more kisses.

Finally it was Erin's turn to give Lance his gift. With the emotion that had been running rampant, she was little nervous, but she'd been planning it for too long.

When she handed it to him, she said, "This present is going to make you emotional. So if you would prefer to wait and open it in private, we would all understand."

"It's okay," Lance said. "I can handle it."

He'd barely gotten the box open when tears sprang to his eyes. She'd folded it specifically so that the quilt square with Lily's Daddy's Girl shirt was on top. He pulled the quilt out of the box and held it close.

"After Lily died, I had quilt squares made of all her special clothes," she said. "But I've never been able to bring myself to put the quilt together and use it. When I saw all the pain you were feeling, especially over Lily bear, I knew I had to do this for you. I needed to give you something of hers to treasure."

He reached his arms out to her and Erin gladly went into them. He held her close, still clutching the blanket.

"I didn't think you could ever get me anything to top any of the gifts you've already given me. But this means everything to me."

As he kissed her, she felt all the love and emotion she'd always wanted from him. He might say that she'd given him the best gift, but she believed she was on the winning end of the deal.

Knowing they had an audience, Erin pulled away and sat next to him. "She'll always be part of us."

Then she reached for a corner and showed it to him. The square read "Big Sister."

"I bought this for her to wear for when I told you about the baby. So there's even a little piece of Noel in this quilt."

He hugged her again and as Erin looked around the room, none of the adults had dry eyes.

"Thank you," he said. "But can I make a request? If we're ever fortunate enough to have another baby, will you let me know right away? I don't want to miss even a moment of our future family."

Shane cleared his throat. "There won't be another baby without another wedding."

"Exactly," Fernando added.

Lance kissed the top of Erin's head. "In time. I intend for us to remarry, and I hope it won't take too long to get to that place. But first we need to finish the counseling we started, and find healing for the wounds that separated us to begin with."

His words confirmed the hope in Erin's heart. He'd come here, looking to make peace with her, and now, she believed they'd both found it. She had no doubt that they would end up remarried and that this time, their marriage would be on a firm foundation that would last a lifetime.

Epilogue

The next Christmas

Erin felt slightly guilty for the gift she was going to give Lance. Technically, she had other things to give him, but yesterday, at the store, she'd had a feeling, so she'd picked it up. They'd only been remarried for a couple of months, but it was enough time that the possibility she hoped for just might be true.

Nicole burst into the kitchen as she was wrapping the item. She did her best to try to cover it up, but Nicole swooped in.

"What's that?"

Erin covered it with the bag. "None of your business. It's a Christmas present. Go away."

"It looks like a pregnancy test."

She'd promised Lance he'd be the first to know. And, actually, she didn't know anything. That was the whole point. They were going to take it together. Well, she was going to take it, but her husband was going to be there, positive or negative, through it all, just like she'd promised.

"I said, it's none of your business."

Leah entered the kitchen. "What's this about a pregnancy test? Who's taking a pregnancy test?"

Erin gave an exasperated sigh, which gave Nicole the opportunity to pull the bag off the test.

"I knew it. Are you pregnant?"

Erin grabbed the test. "I don't know. I haven't taken it. I was going to give it to Lance, in private, and he was going to be the first to know. I promised."

The guys came through the back door then, laughing and brushing snow off one another.

"What did you promise?" Lance said, grinning. But then he saw what Erin had in her hands and the smile left his face. "Is that…?"

Erin stood. "Yes. I picked it up on a whim, and I was going to give it to you tonight when we were alone."

"Why don't you take it now?" Nicole asked. "We're all here. You should take it and let us know."

She was going to kill her sisters. Most specifically, Nicole, but Leah's mischievous grin wasn't helping matters.

Erin looked over at Lance. "It's your present. Your call."

"Might as well take it."

He looked nervous. Like he was afraid to hope. She didn't blame him, they'd been through so much.

She took Lance by the hand then pointed at her sisters and their husbands. "You all stay here. Lance is going to wait for me in the bedroom. I am going to take the test, and he gets to read the results. Then we'll tell you all. And if any of you break the rules and there is a baby, I won't let you hold it when it's born."

Her threat worked, because her sisters nodded. They

all loved babies, and they knew if they made her mad enough, she would make good on her promise.

After Erin took the test, she went to the bedroom and handed it to Lance. It wouldn't show positive or negative for a few minutes, so she grasped his hand. "Whatever the result is, we're in this together."

He nodded and squeezed her hand. "I know. But until I saw that test, I didn't realize how badly I wanted to be a dad again."

She closed her eyes as he held her close to him. She wanted the same thing.

"Baby," he whispered. She opened her eyes and looked down at the results. The big plus sign was unmistakable.

They hugged for a moment, tears rolling down her cheeks. She was glad she'd put her foot down to make this a private moment between her and Lance.

When they came out of the bedroom, Erin couldn't help laughing at the sight of her sisters standing at the foot of the stairs, eagerly awaiting the news.

Lance held up the test. "We're having a baby." His voice cracked as he spoke and her sisters rushed her to hug her.

"This is so exciting," Nicole said. "When I saw the test, I was really hoping for it to be positive, because I want to share this special time with you. Our babies will grow up together and be best friends and—"

Erin stared at her sister. "You're pregnant, too?"

A wide grin filled Nicole's face. "Yes. I just told Fernando this morning."

Leah put her hands on her hips and glared at them. "And now you ruined my surprise. I had a big reveal planned for tonight's dinner to share our news with all of you, so now it won't be as exciting. But what does it matter? We're all having babies. And the Three Sisters Ranch legacy is going to live on."

Erin returned to her husband and he held her tight. When she looked over at her sisters, all snuggled up to their husbands, she was so grateful for the gift they'd been given in inheriting this place.

The door slammed open and the boys raced in, but then they stopped.

"Not this mushy stuff again," Dylan said. "Mom and Dad can't stop hugging and kissing each other. It's kind of gross."

Shane shook his head. "It is never gross for a cowboy to love his wife. The cowboy way is to love your wife with all your heart."

Dylan made a noise. "If having a wife means all that gross stuff, count me out. I'll be the Lone Ranger. Come on, Ryan. Let's go visit the animals."

Lance gave Erin another squeeze. "Marrying you was the best thing I've ever done. Life around here is never dull."

Erin pulled away. "The best thing? No, it was the second best. Marrying you the second time? Now that was the best thing."

He laughed and kissed her again. "I stand corrected."

As they continued their holiday preparations, Erin couldn't help thinking how, each Christmas, life just got better and better. She glanced over at her binder, sitting on the counter. Even though Lance still made fun of her for having her checklist, he couldn't deny that every year together, it was the perfect Christmas.

* * * * *

If you enjoyed this
Three Sisters Ranch story,
be sure to pick up the previous books in
this series to see how Erin's sisters found
their happily-ever-afters:

Her Cowboy Inheritance
The Cowboy's Faith

Available now from Love Inspired!

Dear Reader,

Christmas is a hard season for some people, because while it is supposed to be a time of joy, for some, it is a reminder of pain and loss.

Grief takes many forms, and people express that grief differently. Erin and Lance deal with the loss of their daughter differently, but in the end, the thing they need the most is each other. We are better together when we can share the burdens of our heart.

As you enter the Christmas season, I pray that you will find peace and joy. For those of you who are reminded of your grief this time of year, I pray the Lord will bring you comfort. For those of you who are filled with the holiday spirit, be on the lookout for those who might need a little extra love. If we remember the spirit of love, and share that love with one another, we can make the holiday brighter for everyone.

I love connecting with my readers, so be sure to find me online:

Newsletter: eepurl.com/7HCXj
Website: www.danicafavorite.com
Twitter: Twitter.com/danicafavorite
Instagram: Instagram.com/danicafavorite/
Facebook: Facebook.com/DanicaFavoriteAuthor
Amazon:Amazon.com/Danica-Favorite/eB00K-RP0IFU
BookBub: bookbub.com/authors/danica-favorite

May the blessings of the Lord be with you,
Danica Favorite

COMING NEXT MONTH FROM
Love Inspired®

Available November 19, 2019

AN AMISH CHRISTMAS PROMISE

Green Mountain Blessings • by Jo Ann Brown

Carolyn Wiebe will do anything to protect her late sister's children from their abusive father—even give up her Amish roots and pretend to be Mennonite. But when she starts falling for Amish bachelor Michael Miller, can they conquer their pasts—and her secrets—by Christmas to build a forever family?

COURTING THE AMISH NANNY

Amish of Serenity Ridge • by Carrie Lighte

Embarrassed by an unrequited crush, Sadie Dienner travels to Maine to take a nanny position for the holidays. But despite her vow to put romance out of her mind, the adorable little twins and their handsome Amish father, Levi Swarey, soon have her wishing for love.

THE RANCHER'S HOLIDAY HOPE

Mercy Ranch • by Brenda Minton

Home to help with his sister's wedding, Max St. James doesn't plan to stay past the holidays. With wedding planner Sierra Lawson pulling at his heartstrings, though, he can't help but wonder if the small town he grew up in is right where he belongs.

THE SECRET CHRISTMAS CHILD

Rescue Haven • by Lee Tobin McClain

Back home at Christmastime with a dark secret, single mom Gabby Hanks needs a job—and working at her high school sweetheart's program for at-risk kids is the only option. Can she and Reese Markowski overcome their past...and find a second chance at a future together?

HER COWBOY TILL CHRISTMAS

Wyoming Sweethearts • by Jill Kemerer

The last people Mason Fanning expects to find on his doorstep are his ex-girlfriend Brittany Green and the identical twin he never knew he had. Could this unexpected Christmas reunion bring the widower and his little boy the family they've been longing for?

STRANDED FOR THE HOLIDAYS

by Lisa Carter

All cowboy Jonas Stone's little boy wants for Christmas is a mother. So when runaway bride AnnaBeth Cummings is stranded in town by a blizzard, the local matchmakers are sure she'd make the perfect wife and mother. But can they convince the city girl to fall for the country boy?

SPECIAL EXCERPT FROM

Love Inspired®

Carolyn Wiebe will do anything to protect her late sister's children from their abusive father—even give up her Amish roots and pretend to be Mennonite. But when she starts falling for Amish bachelor Michael Miller, can they conquer their pasts—and her secrets—by Christmas to build a forever family?

Read on for a sneak preview of An Amish Christmas Promise *by Jo Ann Brown, available December 2019 from Love Inspired!*

"Are the *kinder* okay?"

"Yes, they'll be fine." Uncomfortable with his small intrusion into her family, she said, "Kevin had a bad dream and woke us up."

"Because of the rain?"

She wanted to say that was silly but, glad she could be honest with Michael, she said, "It's possible."

"Rebuilding a structure is easy. Rebuilding one's sense of security isn't."

"That sounds like the voice of experience."

"My parents died when I was young, and both my twin brother and I had to learn not to expect something horrible was going to happen without warning."

"I'm sorry. I should have asked more about you and the other volunteers. I've been wrapped up in my own tragedy."

"At times like this, nobody expects you to be thinking of anything but getting a roof over your *kinder*'s heads."

He didn't reach out to touch her, but she was aware of every inch of him so close to her. His quiet strength had awed her from the beginning. As she'd come to know him better, his fundamental decency had impressed her more. He was a man she believed she could trust.

She shoved that thought aside. Trusting any man would be the worst thing she could do after seeing what Mamm had endured during her marriage and then struggling to help her sister escape her abusive husband.

"I'm glad you understand why I must focus on rebuilding a life for the children." The simple statement left no room for misinterpretation. "The flood will always be a part of us, but I want to help them learn how to live with their memories."

"I can't imagine what it was like."

"I can't forget what it was like."

Normally she would have been bothered by someone having sympathy for her, but if pitying her kept Michael from looking at her with his brown puppy-dog eyes that urged her to trust him, she'd accept it. She couldn't trust any man, because she wouldn't let the children spend their lives witnessing what she had.

LIEXP1119